DISNEP
ADVENTURE
STORIES

Disney PRESS

New York

TABLE OF CONTENTS

Michael, and Wendy Darling were following him around Never
Land. Before long, they came to a stream.

"Let's cross it the fun way!" Peter suggested.

He grabbed a rope, swung out over the water, and landed
on the other side. One by one, his friends followed, until only
John was left.

"Tallyho!" John cried, and he leaped for the rope. He missed it and fell into the stream with a splash!

As Michael helped him out of the water, John grumbled, "Why does Peter always have to be in charge? Just once I'd like to do things my way!"

When they rejoined the group, John decided he wanted to show Peter how brave and clever he was. A little farther down the trail, he had an idea. "By Jove," he cried, "I've got it!"

"Got what?" asked Michael.

John said, "You'll see." He took Michael's hand, and together they slipped off into the forest.

John and Michael disguised themselves as pirates, hopped in a small boat, and began to row toward a pirate ship that was anchored in the harbor. But it wasn't just any ship—it was Captain Hook's! He and Peter Pan were sworn enemies!

"Where are we going?" asked Michael.

"To spy on Captain Hook!" John said excitedly. "We'll take the information back to Peter."

As the boys reached Hook's ship, they heard a noise. *Tick tock!*

"What's that?" asked Michael. Just then, a pair of beady eyes poked up out of the water. It was the Crocodile. Once, he'd swallowed an alarm clock, and now he always made a ticking sound.

"Be careful!" John warned. But he didn't have to worry. Years ago, the Crocodile had eaten Captain Hook's hand, and ever since, the pirate was the only person he had chased.

John and Michael had just climbed over the side of the ship when they heard footsteps. John spotted two mops and a bucket. He whispered to his brother, "Pretend you're washing the deck."

A moment later, Smee, the first mate, came around the corner. "Ahoy, mateys!" he called. "Can't say that I remember you. But whoever you are, you're doing a fine job!"

When Smee was gone, John turned to Michael and said, "Come on, we've got some spying to do. I'm going to look for Hook." He found a telescope and climbed up the rigging.

Smee walked by again. "Do you see anything?" he asked.

"Uh, a storm, actually!" John blurted out.

"I should tell the captain," Smee replied. He hurried off.

John turned to Michael. "This is perfect. He'll lead us right to Captain Hook!" They followed Smee at a safe distance and saw him enter a cabin. "Stand watch. I'll be right back," John whispered to his brother.

When John peered through the porthole of the cabin, he saw Captain Hook. Unfortunately, the pirate also saw him. Unlike Smee, Hook could tell that John was not a real pirate.

"Spies!" thundered Hook. "Get them, Smee!"

"We're doomed!" Michael cried.

"Not necessarily," said John.

The first mate came scuttling out of the cabin. When he saw the boys, he said, "Oh, it's you!"

"Indeed it is," said John. "We've been checking the safety of the captain's quarters, and I must say that we're shocked. Why, spies could look through that porthole as easily as I did!"

Smee led the boys inside. "What's the meaning of this?" Captain Hook demanded.

The first mate stammered, "Th-they say they were checking on your safety, sir. And I must say, they're hard workers. Just today I saw them swabbing the deck and standing lookout."

The captain looked John straight in the eye. "Yes," he agreed. "I think they're doing a fine job. After all, with the attack only three days away, security is more important than ever."

"Attack?" said John.

Hook said, "Yes, on Peter Pan's hideout." He turned to his first mate. "Release them, Smee. We've got work to do."

As soon as the boys were outside, John whispered to Michael, "We have to warn Peter!" Quickly, they climbed over the side of the ship and began rowing toward shore.

Captain Hook laughed as he watched through his telescope. "They'll lead us straight to Pan!" he said.

Smee straightened his glasses and looked at Hook. "Y-you mean, they really *were* spies?"

"Of course," the pirate replied. "They're some of Pan's little friends. They don't know it, but now they're working for us!"

A short time later, John and Michael reached the shore. "My plan worked!" John cried. "Wait till Peter hears!"

"Uh-oh," Michael said. "I hear ticking. Like a clock. Like a clock in a crocodile. Like a clock in a crocodile that follows Captain Hook!"

The boys looked at each other. "Hook?" they said. "Run!" They scrambled up a hill, with John leading the way. When he reached the top, he called, "This way, Michael!"

But there was no answer. . . .

"Michael?" John asked, looking over his shoulder.

Captain Hook was standing at the bottom of the hill. Beside him, two pirates had Michael in their clutches.

"Keep going, John!" cried Michael. "Don't stop!"

A few minutes later, John burst into Peter's hideout. "Come quick!" he yelled. Peter, Wendy, and the others gathered around him. John told them what had happened to Michael and that Hook was planning to attack.

Peter shook his head. "If Hook knew where I lived, why would he have followed you? I think it was a trick."

"He knew Michael and I weren't pirates?" asked John.

"I'm afraid so," Peter said.

John groaned. "I've made a terrible mess of things. Will you help?"

"Sure. I've got a plan," Peter replied. "Let's go!"

On the pirate ship, Smee tied Michael to a chair, while Hook tried to find out where the secret entrance to Peter's hideout was.

Just then, they heard a girl's voice say, "Captain Hook?"

It was Wendy. She was standing on the ship's plank. "Watch the boy, Smee," Hook said. "I'll be right back!"

As soon as Hook was gone, John looked into the porthole.

"Not you again!" Smee exclaimed and chased after John.

The Lost Boys hurried inside and untied Michael. Then they climbed down into a boat that was waiting below.

When the boys were all safe, John opened his umbrella, leaped over the side of the ship, and floated down to join them. Then the Lost Boys cast off and headed for shore.

Meanwhile, on the ship's plank, Captain Hook reached out to grab Wendy. Suddenly, a green blur streaked through the air and scooped her up. It was Peter Pan!

"Blast you, Pan!" Hook cried. He lunged forward and fell overboard, snagging the plank with his hook. "Smee!" Hook cried as the Crocodile circled below.

Later that evening, Peter and his friends sat in their hideout, talking about the rescue.

"When Michael and I met Captain Hook, how did he know we weren't pirates?" asked John.

"Pirates don't usually carry umbrellas," Peter said, smiling.

Everyone laughed. What an adventure they'd had!

Buzz's Backpack Adventure

Andy raced down the stairs. It was space day at school, and he couldn't wait to get there. He and his classmates were going to learn all about the planets and the solar system.

"I know!" Andy cried. "I'll bring Buzz Lightyear with me." Then he put the space ranger in his backpack and poured himself a bowl of Space Flakes.

After breakfast, Andy set off for school.

Wow, a whole day devoted to space, Buzz thought. That will be amazing! Plus, I'll get to see where Andy goes to school.

In class, the teacher taught Andy and the other students about the solar system. They also learned that the planets revolved around the sun and that Jupiter was the largest planet.

Brring! The lunch bell rang. Andy and his friends went to the cafeteria. Once they were gone, Buzz looked around and stepped out of the backpack. It was time to explore!

He saw models of the stars and planets hanging from the ceiling. Then he spotted a large cage. A hamster was inside, but

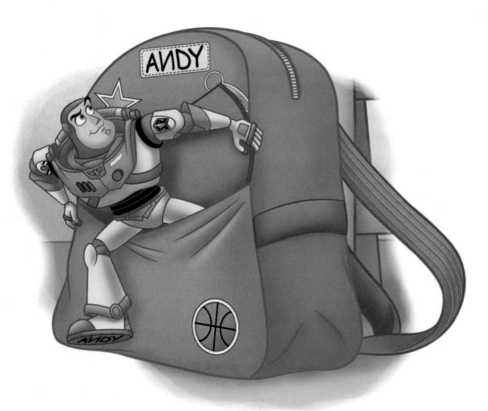

Buzz hadn't ever seen one before. He walked over to it. "Greetings, strange creature," he said. When the hamster didn't reply, Buzz lifted the lid off the cage so he could go inside and get a better look.

Just then, the hamster jumped out of the cage. It ran into Buzz and sent him flying.

Luckily, Buzz noticed some planets dangling in the air above him. He quickly grabbed onto one so he wouldn't fall on the floor.

"Come back!" Buzz cried as the hamster ran away. "I mean you no harm."

Then, all of a sudden, he lost his grip and—*splat!*—fell into a jar of paint.

"Blast!" Buzz cried. He was covered in blue paint. I better clean up before I rescue the creature, he thought.

A few minutes later, Buzz began to look inside the students' desks. He found old chewing gum, broken yo-yos, and moldy sandwiches, but no sign of the hamster. "Blech!" he cried. "There's no way a creature would want to hide in here."

He put down the desktop and made his way over to a table.

There, he spotted some creatures from space!

Or at least, he thought they were from space. They were actually aliens that Andy and his classmates had made from clay. "Greetings," Buzz said. "Have you seen a strange, furry creature?"

When the clay aliens didn't answer, Buzz shook hands with one of them to show that he was friendly. Its arm fell off.

"Sorry about that!" Buzz cried. He set the arm down and jumped off the table . . . straight onto a tower of blocks. Oops, Buzz thought as it wobbled back and forth. Then—*crash!*—the tower came tumbling down.

Buzz noticed that the classroom was a mess. Paint and blocks were all over the place, and the hamster was still on the loose. Buzz knew he had to clean up—and fast!

Brring! The bell rang just as he was stepping back into Andy's backpack.

Buzz looked at the cleaned-up classroom. No one will ever know what happened, he thought.

When the class returned, it was time for show-and-tell. "This is Buzz," Andy said. "He's the best space ranger ever!"

Suddenly, Andy's classmates pointed at the chalkboard ledge. The hamster was sitting on it.

"How did you get out?" the teacher asked as she brought it back to its cage.

The hamster smiled at Buzz. He smiled back. He couldn't wait to tell Woody and the others about his exciting day. . . .

WALT DISNEY's
101 DALMATIANS

Lucky's Busy Afternoon

Perdita and Pongo looked over at their puppies, who were curled up together in a sleeping basket. The two Dalmatians were going to a neighborhood party with their human pets, Roger and Anita. It was a beautiful day, and Pongo was very excited. But he knew Perdita was worried. "We won't be gone long," he promised.

"I'm just not sure we should leave the puppies," Perdita replied. "Will Nanny be able to handle all fifteen of them by herself?"

Pongo smiled at his little Dalmatians. They were sound asleep. "What could possibly go wrong?" he asked. "The puppies are napping. Besides, Nanny can handle anything."

Perdita nodded and followed Pongo outside. He's right, she told herself firmly—the puppies will be absolutely fine. They'll probably just sleep all afternoon.

Before long, Rolly's paw hit Pepper's ear and woke him up. Then Patch nudged Lucky. A few minutes later, all fifteen puppies were awake. They yawned and stretched.

The smell of fresh summer air made them want to go outside. "Let's get Nanny to take us for a walk!" Lucky said to the other puppies.

"That'd be fun!" cried Patch.

"Yeah, good idea!" Rolly added.

A couple of the puppies grabbed a leash that was next to the basket. Then they all yipped as loudly as they could and waited for Nanny to come over.

When Nanny heard
the puppies barking, she went
to see them right away. "Oh, dear," she
said as she looked into their big, hopeful
eyes. "You look like you want to go outside."

The puppies scampered out of the basket
and Nanny scooped them up. "I don't think
Pongo and Perdita would mind if we went for a
walk," she said.

Soon Nanny and the Dalmatians were on their
way. "Let's go to the playground," Nanny said. "It's the
perfect spot for pups to play."

When they got there, Nanny unhooked the puppies' leashes.

The Dalmatians began to run around. It was a beautiful day!
Patch and Pepper dug a hole in the sandbox. Rolly found a rope
to chew on.

Lucky spotted a pretty butterfly. He got ready to pounce, but the butterfly flew up to the top of a slide. Lucky ran up the steps, hoping to catch the beautiful creature.

It flew to a nearby wall, so Lucky jumped from the slide and landed next to it. As the butterfly flew away again, Lucky barked at it. *Woof! Woof!*

His brothers and sisters didn't hear him because they were busy playing. They were so busy, in fact, that they didn't notice when Lucky jumped down to the other side of the wall.

But Lucky didn't land on the ground. He had jumped onto the back of a fire truck! It started speeding down the road.

Woo! Woo! the sirens blared.

Woof! Woof! Lucky barked. "I'm a fire dog!"

Soon the truck pulled to a stop. The firefighters got the ladder from the back of the truck and set it up next to a big tree.

A kitten was stuck in one of the branches. Lucky barked at it to come down, but it didn't understand. Lucky didn't want to make the kitten more nervous, so he jumped off the truck. It was time to go back to the playground anyway.

On his way back, Lucky saw a little girl with curly red hair pushing a doll carriage. "A puppy!" she exclaimed. She reached down and picked him up. "You can be my new dolly," she said. Then she tied a bonnet to Lucky's head and dropped him into the carriage. "I'm going to keep you forever."

Grrr, Lucky growled. He did not like being a doll. Besides, he had to get back to his family!

Suddenly, the little girl spotted something on the ground. "A button!" she cried. She bent down to pick it up. Lucky knew there was no time to lose. He jumped out of the carriage and used his paws to get the bonnet off. Then he ran down the street as fast as he could. At the end of the block, Lucky cocked his ears and listened. He could hear barking!

He raced across the street. *Beep! Beep!* A horn honked at him. He jumped back, and a car went roaring by—right through a mud puddle. Dirty water splashed all over Lucky, but he ran on. When he finally made it to the playground, he was out of breath.

Inside the playground, Nanny was trying to count the puppies, but they wouldn't stay in one place.

"Oh, I give up!" she said finally.

Woof! Woof! Lucky barked as he scratched eagerly at the gate.

Nanny looked up. "Why, hello, little pup," she said as Lucky wagged his tail. "Too bad you can't come with us, but you're not a Dalmatian. You should go find your own family—I'm sure they're worried about you."

43

Lucky was confused, but then he caught sight of his reflection in a nearby puddle. He was covered with dirt. He looked like a Labrador puppy—no wonder Nanny hadn't recognized him!

Then he heard some children laughing. He followed the sound and saw them playing in a fountain.

That's perfect, Lucky thought. He ran over and jumped in.

The children giggled and chased him around. "Look, he has spots," one of them said.

Lucky knew he must be clean. He got out of the fountain and shook his wet fur. A man sitting on a nearby bench looked over and frowned.

Better get out of here! Lucky thought. He ran home as fast as he could. Nanny was outside the house, unhooking his brothers' and sisters' leashes.

"My goodness," she said as Lucky ran past her and into the house. "Where did you come from?"

Later, when Pongo and Perdita came home, they found Lucky curled up in the sleeping basket.

"You see?" Pongo whispered to Perdita. "They're all here. I told you nothing would go wrong. Lucky's even asleep again. He must have had a wonderful afternoon."

Disney's

The Three Musketeers

All for One

Once upon a time, there lived three young friends named Mickey, Donald, and Goofy. They dreamed that someday they'd be musketeers—brave soldiers who lived by the words "All for one and one for all!"

When they grew up, Mickey, Donald, and Goofy got jobs at Musketeer Headquarters. They hoped that if they did good work, Captain Pete, head of the musketeers, would notice them.

Captain Pete *did* notice them—when they broke a water pipe while he was taking his monthly shower! He burst into the cellar and scowled at them. Mickey's dog, Pluto, whimpered. He could see how angry the captain was.

"W-w-we want to be musketeers, so we were practicing our teamwork," Mickey explained.

Pete just laughed. He knew they'd never be musketeers. Mickey was too small, Donald was a coward, and Goofy was— well, goofy.

The three friends went back to work, hoping their luck would change.

Meanwhile, Captain Pete decided he wanted more power. He came up with a plan to become king of France. He would kidnap Princess Minnie, then he would get one of his men to impersonate her and announce that Pete was the new king!

Before Pete could do anything, Princess Minnie asked him to pay her a visit. She was planning to travel more and wanted musketeer bodyguards.

Pete knew that *real* musketeers would interfere with his plan. Luckily, he had an idea. He smiled slyly. "I've got just the men for you, Princess," he promised.

He went to see
Mickey, Donald,
and Goofy.
"Congratulations,"
he said. "You
three have
what it takes
to be musketeers!"

The three
friends couldn't
believe it. Their dreams had
come true! Mickey shouted, "All for one . . ."

". . . and two for tea," Goofy finished.

Mickey laughed. "It's 'one for all'!" he exclaimed. "Now that
we're real musketeers, that's our motto!"

Pluto barked happily.

Later, Captain Pete presented his three new musketeers to Princess Minnie and told her that they would keep her safe.

Just after he left, Minnie's attendant, Daisy, walked in carrying a tray with some biscuits, cheese, and a knife.

"Knife!" shouted Goofy.

"Get her!" yelled Donald.

The Three Musketeers tackled Daisy and wrestled the knife away from her.

"Aaaah!" Daisy cried.

"Stop it!" Princess Minnie ordered.

The new musketeers stopped fighting and hung their heads in embarrassment. They hadn't gotten off to a very good start. . . .

Later that day, the princess decided to go to town with Daisy. The Three Musketeers rode with them.

Pete decided it was the perfect time to kidnap Minnie. He sent the Beagle Boys to do the job. They hid on a tree branch and waited for the royal coach to pass by. When it did—*bam!*—they jumped onto its roof.

Mickey and Goofy were ready to fight, but Donald jumped inside the coach.

"Get back out there!" Minnie scolded Donald. She pushed him out, but he landed in a mud puddle. He watched as Mickey and Goofy tried to fight off the Beagle Boys.

The kidnappers quickly outwitted Goofy, and little Mickey was no match for the big bullies. Soon, the musketeers had been defeated.

The Beagle Boys captured the coach—and Princess Minnie and Daisy!

As the Three Musketeers watched the coach speed away, Mickey said, "Pete made us musketeers, remember?"

His friends nodded.

"Then let's go save the princess!" Mickey shouted. The Three Musketeers quickly ran after the coach. They found it in front of a deserted tower. Mickey and Donald pulled on the tower door, but it wouldn't budge.

"Gawrsh, why don't I try?" Goofy suggested. He charged into the door as hard as he could. *Bam!* It swung open.

With Mickey and Donald close behind, Goofy ran up the stairs. He pushed the kidnappers out of a window and into the river below.

Then the Three Musketeers escorted the ladies back to the palace, where Goofy stood guard.

56

Pete wasn't going to give up that easily, though. He sent his lieutenant, Clarabelle, to lure Goofy away.

"Musketeer Goofy," she called, "I am in need of your assistance!"

Goofy walked straight out of the palace, toward the voice. Clarabelle tackled him at once.

Meanwhile, Donald was patrolling the palace as well. He spotted the Beagle Boys and bravely drew his sword.

Then the Beagle Boys drew their weapons. There were so many that Donald got scared and hid inside a suit of armor.

While the musketeers were distracted, Pete captured Minnie and Daisy. Luckily, Donald saw them.

Mickey had been patrolling in another wing of the castle when he heard a commotion. He found Donald, who told him that Pete had kidnapped Princess Minnie and Daisy.

Mickey was shocked. "But he made us musketeers."

"It was all a lie!" Donald cried.

"Well, lie or no lie, musketeers don't run from danger," Mickey began. "And as long as we wear these uniforms, neither do we."

But Donald was still scared. He gave Mickey his uniform and left.

"Well, well, well, if it ain't the One Musketeer," Mickey heard a voice say.

Bravely, Mickey turned around. It was Captain Pete! "By the power vested in me as a musketeer, I arrest you!" Mickey cried.

Pete laughed and captured Mickey. Then he brought him to an island prison and chained him to a wall. "Looks like this is the end of the line," he told Mickey.

"My pals will rescue me," Mickey shot back.

"Face it!" Pete yelled. "You're on your own! And now I'm leaving for the opera, where I'll become king." Then he pulled the cap off a nearby pipe. Water suddenly began to pour into the dungeon. Soon it would be flooded!

Mickey wasn't the only one in danger, though. Clarabelle still had Goofy in her clutches and was about to throw him off a bridge!

The bridge railing gave way, and Goofy fell over the edge. Luckily, Donald was in a boat just below. He and Pluto had been searching for Goofy.

The boat sank, but they made it to the riverbank. Goofy knew they had to save Mickey. "It's all for one and one for all," he reminded Donald, who was still scared. Pluto barked in agreement.

In the dungeon, the water had risen up to Mickey's chin. Just when it looked as if all hope was lost, Goofy and Donald arrived! They quickly freed Mickey and pulled him to safety.

"Thanks, guys," Mickey said.

"When the three of us stick together . . ." Goofy began.

". . . we can do anything!" Donald finished.

Mickey stood up. "Musketeers, we've got a princess to save!"
The three friends raced off to the opera.

When the Three Musketeers got there, two of the Beagle Boys
were carrying Minnie and Daisy out in a large sack. "All right,
you two, drop the princess!" Mickey ordered. The
Beagle Boys drew their swords. The
fight was on!

Meanwhile, the third Beagle Boy, dressed as Princess Minnie, walked onstage. "My loyal subjects," the fake princess said, "I would like to introduce you to the man who will be your new ruler—King Pete!"

The audience was shocked.

Mickey freed Minnie and Daisy and walked onstage.

"It's all over," Captain Pete told Mickey as he stepped onstage, too. "And you're all alone."

Mickey turned around. Goofy and Donald were nowhere in sight. But Mickey knew he could count on his friends—he was sure they'd appear at any moment. Then he heard Donald and Goofy cry, "All for one and one for all!" They burst onstage, still in the middle of a sword fight with the Beagle Boys. The Three Musketeers knocked the stuffing out of Captain Pete. They had triumphed!

Princess Minnie was so grateful that she made the three friends Royal Musketeers!

Mickey, Donald, and Goofy could hardly believe it. They might not have been the bravest soldiers, but by working together, they had succeeded.

As the crowd cheered, Mickey couldn't help but shout, "All for one . . ." Everyone—even Princess Minnie—added, "And one for all!"

Surfing the Jungle

"These bananas are great!" Terk the gorilla said to her friend Tarzan as they sat on the branch of a tall banana tree. "Remember the first time you tried to get your own bananas?"

Tarzan laughed. "How could I forget?" he asked.

Tarzan and Terk smiled as they remembered the day years before, when Tarzan had tried to pick a bunch of bananas all by himself. . . .

Tarzan had been about five years old. He and Terk were exploring the jungle. "You'll never catch me!" Terk cried as she raced ahead.

Tarzan did his best to keep up, but he had a strange shape for a gorilla, and sometimes it slowed him down. The other apes didn't really think Tarzan fit in, but Terk had tried to be his friend since the day Tarzan's ape mother, Kala, had found him.

Suddenly, Terk stopped in her tracks.

Tarzan caught up to her and whispered, "Why did you stop?"

"Can't you smell the bananas?" she asked.

Tarzan inhaled. He couldn't smell anything.

Terk sighed, then pointed above them.

Tarzan looked up. He couldn't see anything, either. "There aren't any bananas up there," he said, folding his arms across his chest.

Terk planted her hands on her hips. "Wanna bet?" she asked. Then, turning to the tree, she scrambled up its thick trunk.

Looking around, Tarzan bit his lip. Terk made it seem as if climbing trees was easy. But it wasn't, at least not for Tarzan. He ran toward the tree and jumped as high as he could. Unfortunately, it was a long way from the top.

Terk laughed and dropped a banana peel on Tarzan's head. "Tarzan, you are one strange gorilla!" she cried.

Tarzan slid to the ground. Now he was even more determined to follow her. He wanted a banana, not just a peel. And he wanted to show Terk that he was just as good a gorilla as she was, even if he looked different.

Tarzan decided to try a different approach. He hugged the tree and tried to inch up the trunk. But he didn't get very far, and after a few moments, he couldn't hold on anymore.

Within seconds, Tarzan fell to the ground. His gorilla mother, Kala, saw him and hurried over. "Why don't you stay with me this afternoon?" she suggested as she picked him up.

Tarzan reached over Kala's shoulder and grabbed a vine that was hanging from the tree next to Terk's. He used the vine to swing himself onto a low branch.

"Terk always says I'm a strange gorilla," Tarzan told his mother. "I want to be like everybody else." Balancing carefully, he stood up and reached for the branch above his head. "That's why I'm going to climb this tree and get a bunch of bananas!"

"Tarzan," Kala said, "you're not strange, you're special."

But Tarzan had already started to pull himself up onto the next branch.

Tarzan grabbed another branch and swung his leg up and over it. He did the same thing, moving from branch to branch until he was almost at the top.

Then he inched his way out on a limb.

"Ho-hum!" Terk yawned, and threw another banana peel at Tarzan. It missed him and fell to the ground.

Tarzan strained to reach the next branch.

"Chirp, chirp!" A group of baby birds stretched their necks to peek out of their nest. Tarzan smiled at them.

"*Aaah!*" Tarzan cried suddenly. A mother bird had just swooped down near him. He stood up, and the thin branch beneath him swayed.

71

Tarzan reached out and grabbed a vine. He used it to swing to the branch just below.

"Oof!" Tarzan grunted as he landed. Just then, he heard a strange noise coming from a large hole in the tree right in front of him. He wondered what it could be.

He peeked into the hole, and his jaw dropped at what he saw there. Bees! *Bzzz! Bzzz! Bzzz!*

"*Aaarrggh!*" Tarzan turned and ran along the branch as the angry bees swarmed out of the hole. He began to slide on the wet moss covering the branch.

Whoosh! Tarzan slid down the tree limb so fast that he quickly left the bees far behind. He felt as if he were surfing.

Soon the branch got smaller. Tarzan tried to slow down before he reached the end, but he was going too fast. He did not know how to stop!

"Help me!" Tarzan cried as he flew right into Terk's tree—but Terk wasn't there anymore. Tarzan landed on another mossy branch and slid past a family of surprised baboons. Then, he hit a bunch of bananas. Clutching the bananas to his chest, Tarzan fell to the ground.

He landed right in the middle of his gorilla family.

"Tarzan, you really *are* one strange gorilla," Terk said.

"Are you okay?" Kala cried. She hurried over and pulled Tarzan to his feet.

"I'm fine," he answered sheepishly.

Kala smiled. "I see you got those bananas you were looking for," she said, picking one out of the bunch. She peeled it and took a big bite. "Delicious!" she exclaimed. "Why, I do believe this is the best banana I have ever tasted! And you've brought back enough for everyone—how thoughtful."

Tarzan, Terk, and Kala walked home, carrying the bananas. Tarzan handed them out to the other gorillas.

"These look really good!" one of the gorillas exclaimed.

"Yeah, thanks!" another cried.

"Terk never brings us bananas," one of the younger gorillas pointed out.

Terk looked embarrassed.

Tarzan laughed. "Have a banana," he said to her.

Terk smiled and took the fruit. "Thanks," she said. "The bananas *do* look good."

"Sure," said Tarzan. "I've never been surfing in the jungle before. I bet I'll always remember it."

". . . And I always have," the grown-up Tarzan said, as he finished the story. He offered some fruit to Terk. "Have a banana," he said, smiling.

"Tarzan," she said with a laugh, "you are one special gorilla."

Disney's
THE GREAT MOUSE DETECTIVE

BASIL SAVES THE DAY

It was Olivia Flaversham's birthday, and she was celebrating with her father in his toy shop. "You know, Daddy, this is my very best birthday!" the young mouse said.

"But I haven't given you your present yet," her father replied. "Close your eyes."

Mr. Flaversham placed a beautiful ballerina doll on the table. It played music and began to dance around.

Olivia's eyes fluttered open. "Oh, Daddy!" she cried. "You made this just for me? You're the most wonderful father in the whole world!"

Suddenly, there was a loud knock on the door. It was awfully late, and Mr. Flaversham felt uneasy. Opening a cabinet door, he whispered to Olivia, "Quickly, dear. Stay in here and don't come out."

While she was inside, Olivia peeked out and saw a scary, one-legged bat. Soon she heard a big commotion and ran out of the cabinet. "Daddy! Daddy! Where are you?"

But Olivia's father was already gone. He'd been kidnapped!

Meanwhile, Dr. David Q. Dawson had just traveled to London for the celebration of Queen Moustoria's sixtieth year on the throne. He was wandering through the streets looking for a room to rent when he heard someone weeping. He followed the sound and found a young mouse in tears. It was Olivia!

"Are you all right, my dear?" asked Dawson. "Come, come, dry your eyes." He handed her a handkerchief.

"I'm trying to find Basil of Baker Street," she explained. She handed him a newspaper article about Basil, the great mouse detective.

"I don't know any Basil," said Dawson, "but I do know where Baker Street is."

Olivia looked at him with hopeful eyes.

"Come with me," said Dawson. "We'll find this Basil chap together."

The two mice soon found the home of Basil of Baker Street and explained that Olivia needed help finding her father.

But the detective wasn't interested. "I simply have no time for lost fathers," he said.

"I didn't lose him," said Olivia. "He was taken by a bat!"

That got Basil's attention. He knew that the bat, named Fidget, was employed by his archenemy, Professor Ratigan! He explained how evil Ratigan was.

Dawson's eyebrows rose. "As bad as all that, eh?"

"Worse!" insisted Basil. "For years, I've tried to capture him, and I've come close. But each time, he's narrowly evaded my grasp. Who knows what dastardly scheme that villain may be plotting even as we speak?"

Olivia was thrilled: the great mouse detective was on the case! Hopefully, she'd see her father again soon.

Later that evening, Basil paced back and forth. "Ratigan's up to something. The question is: what would he want with a toy maker?"

Just then, Olivia screamed! Fidget had appeared in the window. Basil and Dawson raced outside, but the bat was gone.

Luckily, the mice found his hat lying in the street. It was just the clue they needed.

Basil found his friend Toby, a basset hound.

"Now, Toby, I want you to find this fiend!" the detective told him.

Always happy to help, Toby sniffed the hat and set out in pursuit, carrying the mice through the streets of London.

Toby came to a stop in front of a toy shop.

"Splendid job!" Basil told the dog.

The shop was dark and quiet. Inside were human-sized dolls, games, and toys. Basil noticed that mechanical parts were missing from many of the toys. What had Fidget been up to? And what kind of evil scheme was Ratigan plotting?

Olivia wandered over to a pretty doll cradle. Curious, she peeked inside.

Suddenly, Fidget jumped out at her. He stuffed her into a bag and flew toward an open skylight. Basil chased him, even climbing up a tower of toys, but he couldn't catch the bat. Fidget escaped with Olivia!

The situation looked grim. Now Basil and Dawson had to save Olivia *and* her father! Unfortunately, they had no idea where Ratigan's hideout was located.

Basil paced around the toy shop, thinking hard. Then Dawson showed him a piece of paper that Fidget had left behind.

The detective beamed. "Dawson, you've done it! This list is precisely what we need!"

Dawson looked at him, thoroughly confused.

Back at his house, Basil did several experiments on the note. He mixed some chemicals and looked at the note under his microscope.

"Aha!" Basil cried. He explained that the paper had traces of salt water and coal dust on it.

"Salt water? Great Scott!" exclaimed Dawson.

"It proves beyond a doubt this list came from the riverfront area," Basil declared. They decided to head down there.

Dressed in sailor disguises, Basil and Dawson made their way to the riverfront.

"I feel utterly ridiculous!" Dawson complained.

"Oh, don't be absurd," Basil said. "You look perfect."

"Perfectly foolish!" replied Dawson.

"Dawson, stay close, and do as I do," Basil told him.

Before long, Basil spotted Fidget.

"Come on!" cried Basil. "There's not a moment to lose!"

Quickly, Basil and Dawson followed the bat through a maze of drainage pipes. He led them all the way to Ratigan's secret lair.

"Surprise!" yelled Ratigan and his men.

Basil had walked right into a trap! He and Dawson were surrounded. There was no way out. Even worse, Ratigan wanted them dead and had set up an elaborate contraption to make sure they didn't make it out alive.

Ratigan tied Basil and Dawson to a mousetrap. All around them, deadly weapons were rigged to a record player. When the record stopped playing, a rolling ball would cause the mousetrap to spring and set the weapons into motion.

"It was my fond hope to stay and witness your final scene," said Ratigan, "but you were fifteen minutes late, and I do have an important engagement at Buckingham Palace."

"You fiend!" Dawson cried.

Ratigan left quickly. He was sure the mice would never escape.

Basil began to think hard. He calculated the angles and the timing of the trap and came up with a brilliant idea. They would set off the mousetrap early, which would disrupt the flow of the ball and keep everything else from working properly.

"Ready . . . steady . . . *now!*" yelled Basil to Dawson.

The trap went off, and Basil and Dawson escaped!

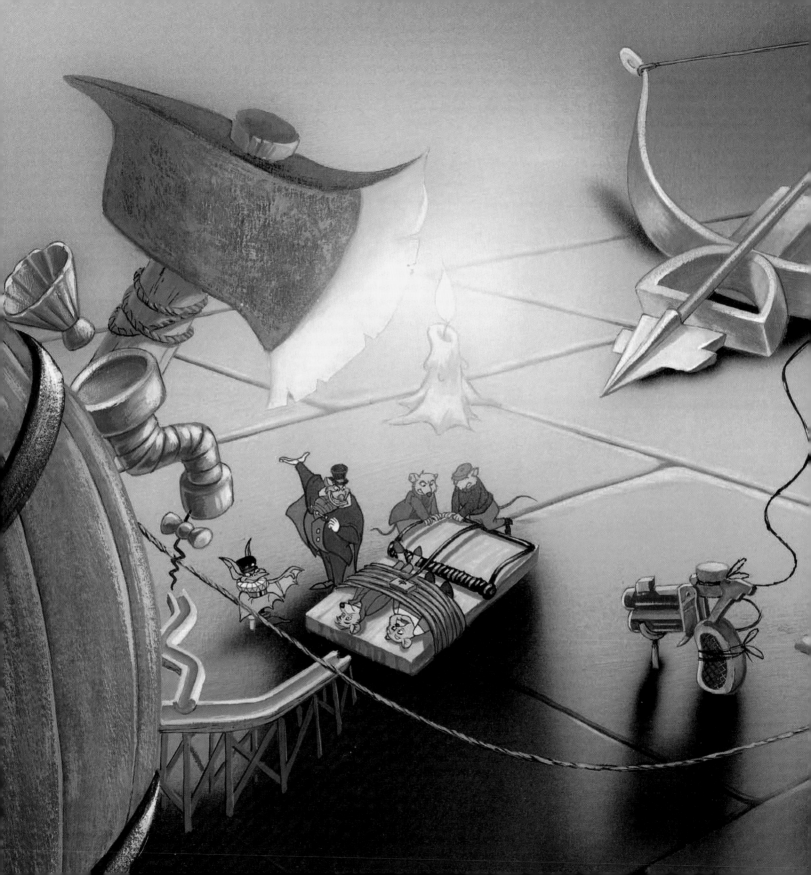

Without a moment to lose, Basil and Dawson found Olivia and raced to Buckingham Palace. There they discovered what Ratigan was up to: he had kidnapped Olivia's father and forced him to build a robot replica of the queen. Once the robot was completed, Ratigan had captured the real queen. He had just replaced Queen Moustoria with the robot.

A huge crowd was listening to the robot queen. "We are gathered here not only to commemorate my sixty years as queen, but to honor one of truly noble stature . . . my new royal consort, Professor Ratigan," it said.

The crowd gasped in horror.

Offstage, Basil and Dawson fought with Ratigan's thugs. Finally, they took control of the robot queen. Basil jammed the controls and caused the robot to malfunction. Ratigan's plan was foiled!

Basil rushed onstage and yelled, "Arrest that fiend!"

After a chase through London, Ratigan was defeated. Best of all, Olivia and her father were reunited. The great mouse detective had saved the day once again!

Disney's
HERCULES
A True Hero

"Hercules! Slow down!" Amphitryon yelled to his teenage son, who was pulling their cart to the market. Their donkey had hurt its ankle, and Hercules had volunteered to lead them the rest of the way. The boy had always been unnaturally strong, so the cart didn't seem heavy. In fact, he was so excited about helping that he was actually running.

"Look out!" Amphitryon called again.

His son was headed straight for a marble archway that was under construction. Because Hercules didn't understand how strong he really was, his attempts to be helpful often turned into disaster.

"*Wh-o-o-a!*" yelled the workmen as Hercules sped through the archway, accidentally knocking them into the air.

Hercules came to a screeching halt in the center of the market. He looked over his shoulder at the workmen, who were hanging from the archway. "Oops," he said sheepishly. "Sorry, guys."

"Heads up!" a voice yelled suddenly.

Hercules looked up and saw a discus flying through the air. "I-I got it!" he called. He leaped into the air and caught it, but the force propelled him right into a pillar. *Smack!*

The pillar began to shake. It swayed. . . . It tottered. . . . Then it hit another pillar. In seconds, all the pillars came crashing down like a set of dominoes!

The townspeople were furious. "That boy is a menace! He's too dangerous to be around normal people!" they insisted.

Hercules felt horrible. If only he could learn to control his strength. If only he could fit in.

That evening, Amphitryon and his wife, Alcmene, decided
to tell Hercules the truth: they weren't his real parents. They'd
discovered him when he was a baby and raised him as their own.

Amphitryon handed Hercules a medallion. "This was around
your neck when we found you," he said. It had a thunderbolt on
it—the symbol of the gods.

Hercules wanted to know more about his past. The next
morning, he left for the temple of Zeus. He
hoped he'd be able to learn whether or not
he was related to any of the gods.

Once Hercules arrived at the temple, he stood before the giant statue of Zeus. Suddenly, a thunderbolt hit the statue and a great stone hand reached down and scooped Hercules up. "My boy. My little Hercules," Zeus said.

Hercules' eyes widened. Zeus, the most powerful of all gods, was his father!

"Didn't know you had a famous father, did you?" Zeus asked.

Sadly, Zeus explained that as a baby Hercules had been stolen and turned into a human. Hercules' superstrength was the only godlike quality he still had.

"If you can prove yourself a true hero on Earth, your godhood will be restored," Zeus told him. "Seek out Philoctetes, the trainer of heroes." With that, Zeus gave a whistle, and a winged horse flew into the temple. It was Pegasus, who had been given to Hercules when he was born.

Hercules jumped on his back. "I won't let you down, Father!" he declared.

That night, Hercules and Pegasus flew to Philoctetes' home. He was a satyr—a half goat, half man—with a reputation for turning ordinary men into extraordinary heroes.

"I need your help," Hercules said. "I want to become a hero, a true hero."

"Sorry, kid," Philoctetes replied. "Can't help you."

"Why not?" asked Hercules.

"I'm too old," the satyr told him.

"But if I don't become a true hero, I'll never be able to rejoin my father, Zeus," said Hercules.

"Zeus is your father?" Philoctetes asked, chuckling. He wasn't convinced at all.

Zap! Zeus fired a lightning bolt at him.

"You win," the satyr told Hercules.

Philoctetes, or Phil as Hercules liked to call him, spent a lot of time training Hercules to become a hero. There were many things Hercules needed to learn.

"Rule number six: when rescuing a damsel, always handle with care," instructed Phil. He tied a doll to a stake and set a fire around it.

Hercules charged in and safely snatched the doll, then ran across a tree that had fallen over a stream. He had almost made it . . . when he tripped. *Splash!* The doll fell into the water.

"Rule number ninety-five: concentrate," Phil coached. He set up a row of targets for Hercules' next lesson.

Hercules threw one sword after another, missing all the targets—and nearly hitting Phil.

"Rule number ninety-six: aim!" Phil said, annoyed.

After many days and a lot of practice, Hercules succeeded with all of his hero lessons. He had grown into a strong, muscular man.

Finally, Hercules felt he was ready to test his strength in the real world. He just had to convince Phil.

"I want to battle some monsters, rescue some damsels," Hercules said. "You know, heroic stuff."

Eventually, Phil agreed. "Okay, okay. You want a road test? Saddle up, kid. We're going to Thebes. It's a good place to start building a reputation."

On the way, they heard a cry for help. Following the sound, they found a centaur—a half man, half horse—holding a girl in his powerful grip.

"Now remember, kid, first analyze the situation," began Phil. "Don't just barrel in there without thinking and—"

But Hercules was already rushing toward the centaur. Using his massive strength, he rammed into the beast headfirst. The centaur crashed into a waterfall. Then—*bam!*—Hercules sent the creature flying with a forceful punch. His first battle had been a success!

Hercules and Phil flew on to Thebes, a city with a lot of troubles. Hercules asked around, eager for a chance to be a hero. But nobody took him seriously.

"We need a professional hero, not an amateur," a woman told him.

Hercules was frustrated. "How am I supposed to prove myself a hero if nobody will give me a chance?" he asked Phil.

Soon Hercules heard that
two boys were trapped in a rockslide
just outside of town. He and Pegasus flew
toward the boys, eager to save them.

Once he got there, Hercules lifted a giant boulder and freed
the trapped children. They were safe! Onlookers clapped and
cheered. Hercules had saved the day!

There was no time to celebrate, though. A terrible monster called the Hydra was emerging from a nearby cave . . . and it was hungry. With a massive head and sharp claws, it went after Hercules.

Hercules ran right and left, successfully avoiding the Hydra's attempts to bite him.

"That's it. Dance around!" called Phil, from a safer distance. "Watch the teeth! *Watch the teeth!*"

With a grunt, Hercules flung a huge chunk of rock at the monster. No luck: the Hydra simply crunched it between its enormous teeth.

Hercules slashed at the monster
with his sword. But when he cut off its head,
many more grew back. The more heads he chopped off, the more
appeared! Soon there were dozens!

"Phil, I don't think we covered this one in basic training!"
Hercules yelled.

Then the Hydra trapped Hercules in one of its claws.
Hercules slammed his arms against a cliff wall with all his might.
Crrrack! Within seconds, the wall broke apart. Huge boulders
tumbled down, killing the monster at once.

Hercules was overjoyed.

"You did it, kid!" cheered Phil. "You won by a landslide!"

The townspeople rushed over and hoisted Hercules on their shoulders. He was a celebrity! Most important, he was well on his way to becoming a true hero.

Disney's
THE EMPEROR'S NEW GROOVE

The Return to the Palace

Once upon a time, there lived a selfish young emperor named Kuzco. He decided to build himself a massive summer getaway called Kuzcotopia. He'd have to destroy a small peasant village to make space for it, but he didn't care. He was the emperor, after all.

Pacha, one of the villagers, was summoned to the palace and told of Emperor Kuzco's plans. He was terribly upset. "What will I tell the village and my family?" he wondered.

Sadly, Pacha loaded his cart and started for home. When he got there, he noticed a strange sack on his cart. He opened it up and peeked inside. A llama peered out. "Where'd you come from, little guy?" Pacha asked.

"No touchy!" the llama cried.

The peasant jumped back. The llama was talking to him! *"Aaaaah!"* Pacha yelled. Then he realized that the llama's voice sounded familiar. It was Emperor Kuzco!

"What happened?" Pacha asked, pointing to the emperor's new hooves.

Kuzco looked down and screamed in horror. "It can't be!" he said in disbelief. He ran to the water trough and looked at his reflection. He had turned into a llama! "My face!" he cried. "My beautiful, beautiful face!"

He demanded that Pacha return him to the palace so that his adviser could make a potion that would turn him into a human again.

But the peasant refused. He was still upset about the emperor's plan to destroy his village. "I can't let you go back unless you change your mind and build your summer house somewhere else," Pacha said.

"I don't make deals with peasants," Kuzco retorted.

"Then I guess I can't take you back," Pacha replied.

The stubborn llama strutted off toward the jungle.

Pacha knew it wasn't safe. "It's a little dangerous if you don't know the way," he said.

But Kuzco ignored him. Before long, he accidentally awakened a pack of sleeping jaguars. *"Aaah!"* he yelled. The jaguars chased Kuzco to the edge of a cliff. He had two choices: jump or be eaten.

Lucky for him, the kindhearted Pacha had followed Kuzco into the dense jungle, knowing the emperor would never survive on his own.

Just when it looked like all hope was lost, Pacha swung in on a vine and grabbed the emperor. Then—*bam!*—they slammed into a tree and got stuck on a branch with the vine wrapped around them.

That was only the beginning of their troubles. . . .

Craaack! The branch soon broke under Pacha and Kuzco's weight. They bounced down the mountain and into a rushing river.

"You call this a rescue?" Kuzco demanded.

"I don't see you coming up with any better ideas," Pacha retorted.

They tumbled and bobbed in the fast-flowing water.

"Uh-oh!" Pacha said suddenly.

They were coming to a waterfall—and they were still tied together. They sailed over the top of it and went flying into the mist. When they finally landed at the bottom, the vine that had been holding them to the log came apart. Pacha and Kuzco quickly floated to the surface, but the llama's eyes were closed. He was unconscious!

"Your highness?" Pacha cried as he dragged Kuzco to shore. Fortunately, the emperor woke up.

That night, Pacha tried once more to convince Kuzco not to destroy his village. "I think if you really thought about it, you'd decide to build your home on a different hilltop," he said.

"Why would I do that?" Kuzco asked.

"Deep down, I think you'll realize that you're forcing an entire village out of their homes just for you," Pacha replied.

The emperor stared at the peasant. "And that's bad?" he asked.

"Unless you change your mind, I'm not taking you back," said Pacha.

The next morning, the emperor said that he would not destroy Pacha's village after all.

The peasant was delighted. He shook Kuzco's hoof and began to lead him through the jungle. They started across an old bridge. Suddenly, some of the boards collapsed!

Pacha fell through a hole and got tangled in a rope. "Help!" Pacha shouted, but Kuzco did nothing to save him.

"I thought you were a changed man," Pacha said.

"I had to say something to get you to take me back to the city," Kuzco replied. "It was all a lie."

As the llama walked off, however, the boards beneath him broke. He fell through the bridge and also got tangled in the rope.

Kuzco and Pacha dangled over the canyon. Pacha was furious that Kuzco had lied to him. And the llama was sick of Pacha. Soon they got into a punching and kicking brawl.

125

Craack! The bridge suddenly broke in half and the ropes snapped. Kuzco and Pacha fell toward the water, but ended up wedged together in a tight crevice.

As alligators circled below, Pacha showed Kuzco how they could work together to inch their way up the gorge, back-to-back. But then, as Pacha reached for the dangling rope that would save them, the llama began to slip.

"Kuzco!" cried Pacha. He grabbed the llama by the tail. Somehow, in a frantic scramble, the llama and the peasant reached the top of the cliff. But in the blink of an eye, the rocky ledge began to crumble beneath their feet. Just in time, Kuzco pulled Pacha onto safer ground.

Pacha stared at the llama in disbelief. "You just saved my life," he said. "There *is* some good in you, after all."

"It was a onetime thing," Kuzco replied.

Pacha decided to take Kuzco back to the palace. Even though he'd been lied to, he'd given the emperor his word. The rest of the journey would take four days.

"I'm still building Kuzcotopia," the emperor said.

"Well, four days is a long time," the peasant replied.

On the way, Pacha and Kuzco stopped at a restaurant. Pacha overheard two of the other people who were there. They were the emperor's advisers. They had turned him into a llama by mistake—they had actually been trying to kill him.

When Pacha told Kuzco, the emperor didn't believe him and got very angry. He told Pacha to leave. The peasant began to go home, but Kuzco soon realized Pacha was right. He caught up to Pacha and apologized.

From that point on, Pacha and Kuzco were a team. They raced to the palace and, working together, they tricked the evil advisers and found an antidote to turn Kuzco back into a person.

Even better, Kuzco realized that he *did* have some good in him. He decided to build Kuzcotopia in a different location, so that he wouldn't have to destroy Pacha's village.

It had been a long trip to the palace, but somewhere along the way, the emperor had found a new groove and changed for the better.

Disney's DINOSAUR

The Long Journey

Aladar's adventure began even before he was born, while he was still inside his shell. When a carnotaur—the most bloodthirsty and ferocious of all the meat-eating dinosaurs—invaded the Nesting Grounds, Aladar's mother had no choice but to flee and leave her eggs behind.

The carnotaur trampled over her nest. All the iguanodon eggs were crushed except one—Aladar's.

The egg soon fell into the greedy hands of another dinosaur, only to be dropped into the river. It was carried away by the current, then scooped up by a pteranodon, a flying dinosaur, who took it across the sea to a distant island.

As the dinosaur flew over the island, the egg was dropped again. This time it fell through the trees and landed on a branch full of lemurs.

Just then, the egg began to crack. . . .

Soon Aladar's tiny face peered out.

"It's a cold-blooded monster from across the sea!" cried Yar, one of the lemurs.

But his daughter, Plio, wasn't so sure. "Looks like a baby to me," she said. Despite her father's arguments, she took Aladar home and raised him as her own.

Time
passed and
Aladar
grew . . .
and grew . . .
and grew. He
was much larger
than all of the
lemurs. But none of them minded—Aladar was part of their
family. Not even Yar could imagine the clan without him. The
young ones loved to play with him, and the older lemurs were
proud that he was so helpful and smart.

Aladar didn't seem to mind the fact that he was the only
iguanodon on the island, either. He was part of a happy family.
"What more could I want?" he asked Plio.

Then, one night, everything changed.

A meteor shower lit up the evening sky. But as the lemurs and Aladar watched, a red-hot boulder—nearly as big as their island—dropped from the stars and into the ocean. A giant cloud of fire and smoke filled the sky. The next thing they knew, a shock wave was speeding toward them, across the boiling sea.

"Run, Aladar! Run!" cried Plio.

With Yar, Plio, her daughter, Suri, and a lemur friend named Zini clinging to him, Aladar ran at full speed away from the terrifying wave. Meanwhile, meteors rained down all around them. Soon it seemed like every bush and tree was on fire.

The island was small, and it didn't take long for Aladar to reach its edge. In front of him and the lemurs was a cliff at least a hundred feet above the water. Behind them, the shock wave was flattening trees and destroying everything in its path.

Aladar and his friends knew what they had to do.

Aladar took a running leap off the cliff just seconds before the shock wave got there.

With his legs churning, the dinosaur fell through the air for what seemed like forever, until at last he hit the water. *Splash!* He and the lemurs found each other, and together they struggled toward the rocky mainland.

Flames raged all around them, and thick, black smoke poured into the sky. Still, they were better off than they would have been on the island, where it seemed nothing was left but fire.

"Come on," said Aladar, rising to his feet and helping the lemurs onto his back. "We can't stay here."

Aladar and the lemurs trudged along for a while, looking for other creatures. Then they spotted a whole herd of dinosaurs! They found out that the herd was marching toward the Nesting Grounds in search of food and water. Aladar and the lemurs decided to join them.

The journey was very long, and Aladar watched as dinosaur after dinosaur collapsed from exhaustion.

The herd's cruel leader, Kron, didn't care. "We stop for nothing!" he growled. "And no one!" As far as he was concerned, weak dinosaurs would be left behind.

But Aladar didn't agree. "If we watch out for each other," he told Kron's sister, Neera, "we all stand a chance of getting to your Nesting Grounds." He did his best to help the young, the old, and the weak carry on, no matter how hard Kron pushed them.

Finding food and water and getting rest were not the only problems the herd had to worry about. A far greater danger emerged—big, mean, *hungry* carnotaurs!

"If we don't keep moving, they'll catch up to us!" Kron growled, pushing the herd even harder.

"But the ones in the back—the young and the old," Aladar argued. "They'll never make it!"

"They'll slow down the predators," sneered Kron. "And if you ever interfere again," he warned Aladar, "I'll kill you!"

Aladar just couldn't stand by and let Kron sacrifice the weakest of the herd. So he and the lemurs stayed behind to help them. Patiently, Aladar tried to hurry the weaker dinosaurs along. But a sudden storm sent them scrambling to a nearby cave.

Bolts of lightning flashed in the sky and thunder crashed around them. *Boom!* Aladar and his friends huddled together, knowing that the herd had moved on. By the time the storm had passed, two hungry carnotaurs had discovered their cave. Aladar and his friends were trapped!

"Do you smell that?" Zini asked.

Suddenly, he leaped over to the far cave wall, and dug at a patch of loose rocks. Soon they gave way, revealing a small opening and a thin ray of sunlight.

"We're out of here!" exclaimed Aladar, charging at the wall.

But instead of making the opening bigger, Aladar started a rockslide that all but blocked it.

"No!" Aladar cried, his heart sinking in despair.

The oldest dinosaur picked up her enormous front feet and slammed them against the cave wall. Immediately, it began to crumble!

The next thing Aladar knew, the weak dinosaurs were breaking down the wall. At last, it gave way, and they found themselves in the Nesting Grounds! But where was the rest of the herd?

Another dinosaur realized that the herd's path had been blocked by an avalanche. Instantly, Aladar knew what he had to do. He raced back through the cave to warn Kron and the herd and show them the new path.

"Listen to him!" Neera urged her brother.

Kron wouldn't listen. Even when a carnotaur appeared, Kron was not about to take anyone else's advice. "This way!" he roared, beginning to climb the steep, rocky wall. "Follow me!"

But the other dinosaurs didn't trust him anymore. They listened to Aladar instead. "Stay together!" he told them. So the herd banded together and bellowed at the carnotaur. Sure enough, it turned away.

Then it spotted Kron all alone . . . and charged!

Kron never did make it to the Nesting Grounds. But thanks to Aladar, the rest of the herd did.

"Welcome home," he declared as he led the dinosaurs and his lemur family into the sunny, green valley. At last, their journey had come to an end.

Aladar was very happy. He and Neera settled down and soon had a baby of their own. His lemur friends were very excited—it was a new beginning for everyone.

DISNEY·PIXAR
MONSTERS, INC.
Boo on the Loose

Sulley was the top Scarer at Monsters, Inc. He worked on the Scare Floor with his one-eyed friend, Mike, who was his scare assistant. Sulley's job was to scare human children. First Mike would set up a closet door for Sulley to walk through. Once a red light came on, Sulley opened the door and stepped into a bedroom. Then he frightened the children inside until they screamed loudly.

Next, Mike captured the screams and sent them to the Monsters, Inc. factory. There, the screams were converted into energy, such as fuel for cars or power for lights. The whole city of Monstropolis used energy from the factory.

One night, Sulley was heading home at the end of his shift.
As he walked past the Scare Floor, he noticed a door was still
out. He thought it was odd, since the doors were usually put away
at night. He opened it and peeked inside to make sure a monster
wasn't still working. "Is anybody there?" he asked. No one
answered, so he closed the door.

"Boo!" something said. It was a little girl—and she was on
the Scare Floor!

"*Aaaah!*" Sulley screamed. Every monster knew that nothing from the human world was allowed into Monstropolis—it was too dangerous for monsters. Recently, a monster had returned from an assignment with a sock stuck to him. A whole squad had been brought in to decontaminate him.

And now, a little girl was in Monstropolis. Sulley knew he had to get her out of there before anyone saw her.

Sulley tried to put the girl back into her room. Every time he thought he had, she sneaked back to the Scare Floor.

"Kitty!" she called to Sulley.

The monster had to do something—fast. If anyone found out about her, he could lose his job!

There was only one monster Sulley could talk to—his best friend and roommate, Mike. So, Sulley put the little girl in a bag and sneaked her out of the building.

When Sulley got to the apartment, he took the girl out of the bag. "Her name is Boo," he explained.

"You named it?" cried Mike. He knew that the girl was dangerous—and that he and Sulley would get in a lot of trouble if anyone found out about her.

Mike came up with a plan. Tomorrow, they would drive her to the park and try to lose her.

That night, Sulley and Mike peeked in on Boo while she was sleeping. She was snuggled up with Mike's teddy bear.

"It's hard to believe she's dangerous," said Sulley.

Mike didn't care how nice she looked. "Hey," he said indignantly, "that's my bear!"

"Don't worry about it," Sulley said.

The next morning, Sulley and Mike made a disguise for Boo:
a monster costume. "Be careful!" Mike cried. "Don't let that kid
touch anything!"

They drove to the park, and Sulley and Mike got out of the
car. When Mike tried to open the door for Boo, he couldn't.
She'd locked herself in!

"We have to get her out!" Mike said angrily.

Sulley had an idea. He found a spare tire in the trunk and squished Mike into the middle of it. Then he rolled it around. "Fun!" he exclaimed, trying to get Boo's attention.

"Yeah, fun," Mike grumbled.

Boo just sat in the car.

Next, Sulley took out the car jack and cranked Mike up and down.

"Whoa!" Mike yelled. "This just keeps getting better."

Boo still didn't come out— she was too busy playing with Mike's bear.

Then Sulley swung Mike around in circles. "Don't you want to play, Boo?" he called.

Boo just waved at them.

156

"What do we do now?" Mike asked.

Suddenly, a monster butterfly flew past the car window. Boo smiled and pointed. Then she opened the car door and ran after it!

The butterfly landed on a fountain, and Boo tried to catch it. But the butterfly was too fast. It flew into the woods— and the little girl followed it.

Mike grabbed Sulley's arm. "Now is our chance, Sulley!" he shouted. "Let's go!" Mike tried to start the car, but it was out of gas.

Sulley didn't care—he missed Boo already. Then he thought
of something! If Mike thought they needed Boo, Sulley could
get her back. "We need to find Boo!" he exclaimed. "Her scream
will start the car." He grabbed Mike's teddy bear and ran into
the woods. "Boo?" he called. "I have your teddy bear. . . ."

Sulley looked and looked, but Boo was nowhere to be found.
Was she gone forever?

"Kitty?" a small voice finally said.

It was Boo!
She ran toward
Sulley and
hugged his leg.

The monster
smiled. She
did not seem
dangerous at all.

Sulley and Boo walked back to the car together.

"You're holding its hand!" Mike cried when he saw them.

Sulley smiled. "I know," he said. "I feel okay, though." He helped Boo into the car. Then he got in, too.

Mike turned to his best friend. "Okay, Sulley," he said. "You are the best Scarer at Monsters, Inc. Do your stuff!"

Sulley looked at Boo. She smiled back at him. He opened his mouth to roar . . . but he couldn't do it. He just couldn't frighten little Boo!

"Just scare it—*now!*" yelled Mike. He banged his head on the steering wheel and hit the horn by accident. *Honk!*

"Ouch!" Mike shouted.

Hee-hee-hee!

Boo began to laugh. She laughed and laughed and laughed.

Suddenly, the engine started! *Vroom, vroom!* Mike and Sulley looked at each other. How had that happened?

Mike looked at Boo. Somehow, her laugh must have started the car. Sulley was right—she didn't seem dangerous.

163

"Okay," Mike said, "she can stay for now. But just remember, that is *my* bear!"

Thunder and Lightning

The race that Lightning McQueen had always dreamed of—the Dinoco 400—was just minutes from starting. The winner would get the Piston Cup trophy and the right to the Dinoco sponsorship. Fame and fortune were on the line, and the rookie race car wanted both.

In the quiet of his Rust-eze trailer, McQueen prepared himself. "I'm faster than fast, quicker than quick," he said. "I *am* Lightning." Finally, he was ready to greet his fans. McQueen flashed his lightning-bolt sticker as he burst out of his trailer. "*Ka-chow!*" he cried.

The cars in the stands honked their horns. They loved this hotshot rookie.

McQueen loved the applause. He wanted to be a superstar, but first he had to beat The King and Chick Hicks.

The King had won more Piston Cups than any other car in history, and Dinoco had been his sponsor for years. Now he was ready to retire. Could he win one last race?

Not if Chick Hicks had his way! He had been chasing The King's tail fin his entire career, always coming in second. He was determined to become the new champion and get the Dinoco sponsorship—no matter what.

The cars went to the starting line. The officials waved the flag. Engines roared and the ground shook. The race cars were off!

Right at the start, McQueen zoomed ahead of Chick. Then—*pow!*—Chick rammed into McQueen and sent him spinning. Chick was set on winning, even if he had to use a few dirty tricks!

As The King took the lead, Chick slammed into another racer. Behind him, cars screeched and skidded.

Crash! Smash! Crunch! The cars piled up.

"Get through *that*, McQueen!" Chick taunted his rookie rival.

Coming up from the rear, McQueen dodged the wreckage. He rode over the top of one car like a skateboard. Then he leapfrogged off another and landed perfectly on the track.

As Chick was getting new tires and gas in pit row, McQueen zoomed past. He wasn't going to make a pit stop—he was a one-man show.

"C'mon, get me out there!" Chick yelled to his crew.

Eventually, McQueen pulled in for a pit stop. His crew sprang into action. They told him he needed new tires, but McQueen ignored them. "No tires, just gas!" the rookie insisted. He didn't have time for tires.

"Looks like it's all 'gas 'n' goes' for McQueen today," the announcer said in disbelief as McQueen roared out of the pit. It was a risky strategy.

Back on the track, the white flag waved. There was only one more lap to go!

"Aw, he's got it in the bag!" the announcer shouted. "We're gonna crown us a new champion!"

The fans went wild. McQueen could taste the victory, until . . .

. . . *Ka-blam!*

"Oh, no!" the announcer yelled. "McQueen has blown a tire!"

Only a hundred feet from the finish, McQueen grunted and hobbled along. He didn't have far to go—he knew he could make it before Chick and The King caught him. Then . . . *ka-blam!*

Another tire blew. The rookie was riding on his rims!

McQueen was only fifty feet from the finish, but The King and Chick were gaining on him. Sparks flew as the rookie's rear rims scraped the track.

"And down the stretch they come!" shouted the announcer.

Chick and The King surged forward as McQueen leaped, hopped, and even stuck out his tongue to try to win by a few inches.

The checkered flag dropped as the three cars crossed the finish line. It was too close to call!

In Victory Lane, Chick approached McQueen and growled, "The Piston Cup—it's mine."

"In your dreams, Thunder," said McQueen.

"What are you talking about—'Thunder'?" asked Chick.

"Hey, you know, because thunder always comes *after* lightning," McQueen said with a smile.

The King drove over to McQueen. He couldn't believe the rookie hadn't listened to his crew. "This ain't a one-man deal, kid," he said.

But McQueen wasn't interested. He had only one thing on his mind: being announced the winner.

At last, the results were in! Incredibly, all three top cars had crossed the finish line at the same time! A tiebreaker race would be held in California in a week.

"First one to California gets Dinoco all to himself," taunted Chick.

Lightning McQueen had a lot to learn, but for now he only cared about one thing—getting to California—and fast. . . . *Ka-chow!*

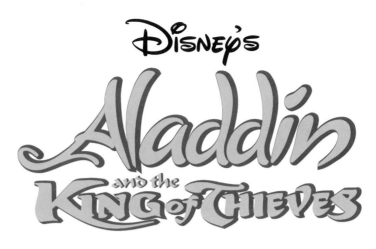

Disney's
Aladdin and the King of Thieves

Treasure Lost, Treasure Found

Aladdin sat in the palace, stunned. He and Princess Jasmine had been about to get married when some of the notorious Forty Thieves burst in. They had tried to steal one of the wedding gifts—the Oracle, a magical scepter that could answer questions about the future and the past.

Aladdin fought the thieves and recovered the Oracle, which surprised him with the news that his father was alive! Aladdin had grown up alone on the streets of Agrabah believing his father was dead.

Jasmine encouraged Aladdin to look for his father. She knew how much it would mean to him to have his father at the wedding. "Take as long as you need," she said.

Aladdin hugged the princess and promised to return soon.

The Oracle had told Aladdin that his father was with the Forty Thieves. Aladdin thought his father had been taken and flew off to rescue him. Aladdin, his monkey, Abu, and Iago the parrot followed the trail of the thieves. They finally caught up with the outlaws at the edge of the sea.

"Open, sesame!" cried their leader. Suddenly, the waters parted like magic. The thieves rode through on their horses and entered a cave on the other side. Aladdin sneaked in behind them.

On the other side of the water, Aladdin found himself inside the thieves' secret lair. He watched them for a few minutes, but soon Aladdin and his father, Cassim, were standing face-to-face. But Cassim was not the thieves' prisoner—he was their leader, the King of Thieves! He was the man who had interrupted Aladdin and Jasmine's wedding!

Aladdin was shocked.

"Like it or not, boy, we are blood," Cassim said.

Sa'Luk, one of the meanest members of the Forty Thieves, didn't care that Aladdin was related to Cassim. "The boy is an intruder!" he insisted. "We have rules about intruders. He has found our secret lair. He has seen too much. He must die!"

Cassim did not want Aladdin to be killed, but he could not appear weak in front of his men. He knew that Aladdin had only one chance for survival. "My son shall face the Challenge," he said.

"What's going on, *Dad?*" Aladdin asked through gritted teeth.

"Oh, the Challenge is simple enough," Cassim said casually. "Only one man survives."

Aladdin realized he was going to have to fight Sa'Luk.

"You're my son—you'll be that man," Cassim said with confidence.

Sa'Luk was strong, but Aladdin was quick and smart. When the thief came after him, he dodged to the right, then the left. Soon the two had battled their way onto a dangerous cliff ledge. Aladdin did not back down and neither did his opponent. Finally, Sa'Luk lost his balance and fell into the water below.

Aladdin sighed with relief and looked up to see his father smiling proudly. Aladdin didn't realize that by surviving the Challenge, he had become a member of the Forty Thieves. He didn't want to be a thief, though. In the morning, he would return to the palace—and Jasmine.

Later that night, Cassim told his long-lost son about a great treasure that he was seeking. It was called the Hand of Midas, and everything it touched turned to solid gold. He showed Aladdin an entire ship that had turned into gold.

Aladdin was angry. So that was the reason his father had left—to search for treasure?

Cassim tried to explain himself to his son. "I knew exactly what I wanted for my family—the best."

"We never wanted gold. We wanted you," Aladdin said. "I wanted a father. I still do. . . . Come to my wedding."

Cassim *did* return to the palace with Aladdin. He met Jasmine, the Genie, and the Sultan. But it turned out he was really only interested in getting the Oracle. He thought it would tell him where to find the Hand of Midas.

When Aladdin found out why his father had come to the palace, he was hurt and angry. He had thought that a different life—and being near him—could change his father.

"You can change my clothes, Aladdin," said Cassim, "but you can't change who I am."

Aladdin said good-bye to his father, who left with the Oracle and Iago to find the treasure.

When Cassim returned to the Forty Thieves' secret lair, he was in for a surprise.

The thieves came out, their swords drawn and faces hardened.

"Why don't they look happy to see you?" Iago asked worriedly.

Cassim saw why: Sa'Luk! He had survived the fall from the cliff and turned the other thieves against Cassim. They took him captive.

Soon after, Sa'Luk tied Cassim and Iago to the mast of a ship, guarded by the other thieves. When they were in the middle of the sea, Sa'Luk demanded that he ask the Oracle the all-important question.

Reluctantly, Cassim asked, "Where can we find the Hand of Midas?"

The Oracle shot out a brilliant white light. "The Vanishing Isle will appear at dawn," it answered. "I will show you the way."

Moments later, Iago escaped from the ship and quickly flew back to the palace. When Aladdin learned that his father was in trouble, he knew he had to help. Cassim may have turned his back on his family, but Aladdin would not make the same mistake.

So Aladdin and Jasmine flew off on the Magic Carpet to rescue his father.

Before long, Aladdin saw a majestic island rise out of the sea on the back of a giant turtle. "The Vanishing Isle!" he said with a gasp. Since the turtle moved around, the island was never in the same place twice.

Once the Magic Carpet landed, Aladdin found his father and Sa'Luk. Jumping from a nearby rooftop, Aladdin tackled Sa'Luk.

"It took me years to find my father," Aladdin said, delivering a swift punch. "I'm not losing him again." Sa'Luk fell to the ground—this time Aladdin had knocked him out.

"You came to help me?" asked Cassim.

"How could I do anything else?" replied Aladdin. "Now, let's get that treasure of yours."

Aladdin and Cassim quickly found the temple that contained the Hand of Midas.

All of a sudden, water came rushing toward them. The great turtle was diving. Soon the Vanishing Isle would be underwater!

Together, they scaled the walls. Then Aladdin jumped, landing on a giant, rotating hand that was floating. On it stood a wooden statue. The statue's hand was gold—it was the Hand of Midas!

"Be careful," Cassim warned Aladdin. "Don't touch the Golden Hand!"

Aladdin grabbed on to the wooden handle attached to the Hand of Midas. He carefully threw the treasure to his father, and Cassim caught it using the inside of his robe. Instantly, that part of the cloth turned to gold!

The temple continued to flood.

"Time to go, Aladdin!" Cassim called out.

"Nobody's going anywhere," said a voice.

It was Sa'Luk. He jumped on the giant floating hand, trapping Aladdin. "Give the Hand of Midas to me, Cassim," he ordered, "or your son dies!"

Cassim threw the treasure to his enemy. Sa'Luk caught it in his hands.

"The Hand of Midas is mine!" he yelled with an evil laugh.

Suddenly, Sa'Luk realized his mistake—he had touched the golden part of the Hand, not the wooden handle. He turned into a golden statue and fell like a stone into the water below.

Aladdin and Cassim carefully recovered the treasure and scrambled to escape the rising water. When they were safe, the King of Thieves took one last look at the Hand of Midas.

"This wretched thing almost cost me the ultimate treasure," said Cassim. He hugged Aladdin. "It's you, son. *You* are my ultimate treasure. I'm sorry it took me this long to realize it. The Hand of Midas can take its curse to the bottom of the sea!" Then he threw the Hand of Midas from the temple roof.

Aladdin and Cassim hurried back to the Magic Carpet. Aladdin turned to Jasmine. "Let's go home," he said. "We have some unfinished business."

Aladdin and Jasmine returned to Agrabah so they could finally get married.

Cassim hid in the shadows and watched his son walk down the aisle. Iago flew up to him. "Broad daylight? No mask? Pretty risky, if you ask me," the bird said.

"Even a 'wanted man' can risk a bit to see his own son's wedding," replied Cassim. He knew Aladdin was well worth it.

On the Hunt

Mowgli's life was very different than it once had been. He had been raised in the jungle by a pack of wolves, a fun-loving bear named Baloo, and a protective panther named Bagheera. Now he lived in a Man-village so that he would be safe from Shere Khan, a tiger who hated him.

Life in the Man-village was difficult for Mowgli. He had a hard time following the rules. He was used to the ways of the jungle, and he missed his animal friends. One day when Baloo came to the village to visit, Mowgli returned to the jungle with him.

But Mowgli didn't realize that his new friends, a girl named

Shanti and a young boy named Ranjan, thought he had been captured. Bravely, the pair headed into the jungle to rescue him. They soon found some mango peels that they thought Mowgli had left.

The smug and cunning Shere Khan was looking for Mowgli, too. The Man-cub had embarrassed him once, and now the tiger wanted revenge.

Shere Khan spotted Kaa the snake. Like everyone else in the jungle, Kaa was afraid of Shere Khan.

"Where is he?" the tiger demanded.

"Who?" Kaa replied.

"The Man-cub—Mowgli," said Shere Khan. "I know you know."

"But I don't!" insisted Kaa.

Shere Khan grabbed the snake's throat.

"He'ssss at the sssswamp!" wailed Kaa.

Shere Khan narrowed his eyes, trying to figure out if the snake was being truthful. "He'd better be. For your sake," he replied.

Shere Khan stalked through the jungle. Silently, he parted the reeds in the swamp and gazed around. There was no sign of Mowgli.

"That snake lied to me!" Shere Khan cried. He swiped a paw into the water in frustration.

Just then, a voice above him said, "Now, don't take it out on the water just because you don't like the reflection! I mean, not everyone can be born with such great looks!" The voice belonged to a vulture named Lucky, who was perched on a branch overlooking the swamp.

199

When Shere Khan glared at him, Lucky got down from the branch and moved closer to the tiger. "What's the matter, Stripes? Man-cub got your tongue?" he teased.

The other vultures tried to stop Lucky, but it was no use.

"We heard that kid is here in the jungle, right under your whiskers," Lucky said.

Shere Khan paused. Now he was interested in listening to the big-mouthed vulture.

"They say he's headed downriver with a bear," Lucky added.

Shere Khan set off to find Mowgli. But before he left, he gave Lucky a parting gift: a de-feathering. That'll teach the bird not to make fun of me, he thought.

Meanwhile, Shanti and Ranjan had caught up to Mowgli, but they'd gotten into an argument, and Shanti and Ranjan had stormed off. With Shere Khan on the prowl, Mowgli knew his friends weren't safe, so he went after them.

In a clearing, Mowgli finally spotted Shanti and Ranjan. "There you are," he said. "I'm so sorry. Will you let me explain?"

Shanti didn't move a muscle.

"C'mon," said Mowgli, "at least talk to me."

Eyes wide with fear, Shanti slowly raised her arm and pointed behind Mowgli. When he turned around, Mowgli was face-to-face with Shere Khan—and the tiger was ready to pounce!

"You seem surprised to see me, Man-cub," Shere Khan said menacingly.

Mowgli stepped between his friends and the evil tiger. He had to save Shanti and Ranjan. This was all his fault.

"You humiliated me, Man-cub," Shere Khan continued. "I simply can't let you live."

Mowgli knew the tiger was serious. "Run!" he whispered to Shanti and Ranjan.

Shanti grabbed Ranjan and took off. Then Mowgli threw some dirt into the tiger's eyes and followed them.

Shere Khan shrugged it off with a chuckle and said, "Oh, you're going to try and outrun me." The tiger trailed after the children, but he decided to take his time. He was going to enjoy the hunt.

Mowgli found a safe hiding place for Shanti and Ranjan. Then he ran away, hoping Shere Khan would follow only him. It worked!

Shanti had her own plan, though. "Ranjan, wait here," she said. "I've got to go help Mowgli. I'll be right back. Don't move!"

Ranjan waited for about two seconds. Then he scampered after Shanti.

Mowgli soon came to an ancient stone theater. He ran up the steps as quickly as he could, with Shere Khan at his heels. Before long, Shanti arrived.

In the meantime, Baloo found Ranjan, and the boy told him what had happened. The bear left Ranjan with Bagheera the panther and went to the theater to try to rescue Mowgli and Shanti.

Inside the theater, Shere Khan paced. He knew Mowgli was there, he just had to find him. "No matter how fast you run . . . no matter where you hide . . . I will catch you!" he called out.

Mowgli hid behind a giant brass gong. Baloo and Shanti soon arrived and hid behind two other gongs. Baloo tried to distract Shere Khan by tapping on his gong. The tiger's head snapped around toward the sound, and he went to investigate.

Shanti saw this and began to hit her gong. Then Mowgli realized Baloo and Shanti were there and hit *his* gong. Shere Khan didn't know which direction to go in . . . until *crash!*

Shanti's gong fell to the ground, revealing her hiding place!

Shere Khan laughed and called out, "So, what's it going to be, Man-cub? You . . . or your adorable little girlfriend?"

As the vicious tiger approached Shanti, Mowgli jumped out from his hiding place. "No, don't!" he commanded.

Shere Khan roared and sprang toward Mowgli!

In the nick of time, Baloo tackled Shere Khan. They rolled around on the ground as they fought, but the tiger wouldn't be stopped. He broke free and headed toward Mowgli.

"Mowgli, look out!" Baloo yelled.

The Man-cub grabbed Shanti's hand. "Come on!" he cried.

Shanti took one look at the tiger and quickly followed Mowgli up a set of nearby stairs. They ran as quickly as they could. Shere Khan was catching up fast.

Within seconds, the tiger had cornered Mowgli and Shanti on a ledge. Below them was a pit of boiling lava.

Mowgli looked around. There was only one way out. "Jump!" he yelled to Shanti.

The pair leaped off the ledge. *"Aaaah!"* they screamed. Luckily, they landed on a stone head, but Shere Khan jumped, too, and landed right next to them.

The stone head began to give way under all the weight. Mowgli, Shanti, and Shere Khan fell toward the bubbling lava!

At the last second, Baloo reached down and grabbed Mowgli and Shanti, hauling them up to safety.

Shere Khan, however, was not so lucky. He landed on a rock in the middle of the lava pit. Then the giant stone head crashed down on him! He roared with fury as Mowgli, Baloo, and Shanti looked on in disbelief. The tiger was trapped!

Suddenly a shadow appeared overhead. It belonged to Lucky the vulture, who landed on the mouth of the stone head . . . which was now Shere Khan's prison.

"Helloooo, Stripes!" called Lucky. "You're looking a bit down in the mouth today. Ha, ha, ha!"

Shere Khan clenched his teeth. "Oh, no," he hissed.

"What's the matter?" Lucky teased. "I always said you had a good head on your shoulders!" He laughed, knowing he'd torture the tiger with bad jokes for a long time.

Shere Khan thought that having to listen to Lucky was the worst punishment imaginable.

Soon after, Mowgli, Shanti, and Ranjan returned to the village. Now that Shere Khan was no longer on the hunt, Mowgli could visit the jungle anytime he wanted. Sometimes he even took Shanti and Ranjan along—they had friends in the jungle now, too!

DISNEY's

THE BLACK CAULDRON

The Great Quest

Centuries ago, there lived an evil king who wanted to be the most powerful ruler in the world. His name was the Horned King, and he knew one object would give him everything he desired—the Black Cauldron.

The Horned King ordered Creeper, his second-in-command, to use whatever means necessary to find it.

"Yes, sire," Creeper replied.

Soon after, a lowly pig keeper named Taran and a beautiful
princess named Eilonwy became trapped in the king's castle.
They began to wander through a maze of underground tunnels
to try to find a way to escape.

Eventually, they came to an ancient burial chamber, where
something caught Eilonwy's eye. It was a magnificent sword!
Taran smiled with delight, then picked it up.

Taran and Princess Eilonwy continued to walk through the tunnels. Soon they heard someone yell, "Help!" They followed the sound and came upon a kindly old man named Fflewddur, who was being held captive in another dungeon. As they were freeing him, they heard Creeper and his men out in the passageway.

There was only one thing to do: run!

"Get them!" cried one of Creeper's men. Another cornered Taran. But when the pig keeper's sword touched the henchman's sword, the henchman's weapon fell to pieces. The sword was magical!

The three fugitives tried to find a way out but quickly realized they were trapped.

Taran swung his magic sword toward the drawbridge chain. Sparks flew and the chain broke loose, which sent the bridge crashing down. Immediately, the trio ran to the safety of the woods. They had escaped!

At last, Taran, Eilonwy, and Fflewddur could stop and rest.

Just then, a furry little creature who was looking for food tackled Fflewddur. It was Gurgi. Taran had met him before and wasn't particularly fond of him, but Gurgi liked the pig keeper.

At the moment, Taran had bigger things on his mind. He had found out that the Horned King was after the Black Cauldron, and he knew he had to find it first.

"If we destroy the Cauldron, it will stop the Horned King," Taran explained to the others. "Please come with me."

They all set off, and before long, they learned that the Cauldron was hidden in Morva. Eventually, they arrived at a run-down cottage. Inside lived three witches, guardians of the Black Cauldron.

"Nobody's asked for the Black Cauldron in over two thousand years," said one witch. They weren't about to give up the Cauldron so easily.

Taran held out his magic sword. "I offer my dearest possession in exchange for the Black Cauldron," he said.

The witches loved a bargain, so they readily agreed. The sword instantly disappeared, and the ground began to shake. Dirt and boulders flew through the air, followed by billowing smoke and steam. Then the mighty Black Cauldron rose from beneath the earth.

"Quick! We must destroy it!" cried Taran.

The witches looked on and cackled wickedly. "The Black Cauldron can never be destroyed," one of them said. "Only its evil powers can be stopped."

"But how?" asked Taran.

"A living being must climb into it of his own free will," one of the witches replied. Then she added, "However, the poor duckling will never come out alive."

What would Taran and his friends do?

Unfortunately, there was no time to think about it. The Horned King's men had caught up to them! Gurgi quickly ran and hid behind a tree while the wicked creatures grabbed the Black Cauldron and took it to the castle along with Taran, Eilonwy, and Fflewddur.

Trembling, Gurgi made his way to the castle. He was terrified, but he knew he could not abandon his friends.

Inside the castle, the Horned King was using the Black Cauldron to bring an evil army of skeletons to life.

"Arise!" the king commanded of his new army. "Our time has arrived! Go destroy all in your path!"

The skeleton army marched out of the castle, but Gurgi sneaked past them. He found his friends and quickly untied them.

The friends were thrilled they had been rescued. Still, Taran knew the kingdom would not be safe as long as the Cauldron's powers were intact. He decided to jump into the bubbling cauldron, even if it meant he would never come back.

"No! You can't!" cried Eilonwy.

"There *must* be another way!" Fflewddur insisted.

Taran shook his head. Bravely he said, "My mind is made up. If I don't, we're all lost."

But Gurgi had other ideas. "Gurgi not let you jump into cauldron!" he said to Taran, blocking his path.

"Get out of my way," Taran said.

Gurgi stood his ground and then jumped into the boiling cauldron himself!

"No!" Taran cried.

But it was no use. Gurgi was gone. Taran couldn't believe he'd been so wrong about the little creature.

The Cauldron immediately began to lose its power. Outside the castle walls, the king's skeleton army collapsed into a heap of bones.

Inside, a mist of vapors swirled around. Torches on the walls blew out, and the gusting wind sucked everything bad into the Cauldron . . . including the Horned King!

The evil ruler was finally defeated!

The strong pull of the Cauldron caused the castle floor to fall to pieces. Roaring flames shot up at Taran, Eilonwy, and Fflewddur as they ran for their lives.

Suddenly, Eilonwy spotted an old boat in an underground canal. They quickly hopped on and rowed to safety as the castle crumbled to the ground. Then the Black Cauldron appeared, bobbing in the water, and the friends remembered poor little Gurgi.

The three witches saw the Black Cauldron, too. They wanted it back. They offered Taran the magic sword in exchange for the Cauldron, but he said no.

"I would trade the Cauldron for Gurgi," said Taran.

"Oh, dear," said one witch.

"It's not possible," said another.

Fflewddur piped up. "Just as I thought," he said to the witches. "You have no real power. Admit it."

The witches were very angry. They decided to show Fflewddur just how wrong he was. They changed into glowing colors and whirled around the Cauldron, lifting it out of the water. As it rose, it was transformed into brilliant white light.

"We have made a bargain!" announced one of the witches.

When the whirlwind dissolved, the Cauldron was gone, the witches were gone, and Gurgi was lying on the ground.

He reached a small paw toward Taran.

"Gurgi," cried Taran, "you're alive!"

With joy, Taran and Eilonwy hugged their hero.

"Gurgi's happy day!" said the little creature as he jumped into Taran's arms.

It was a happy day indeed—for Gurgi, his friends, and all the land.

Adventure in the Outback

Deep in the Australian outback there lived a young boy named Cody. He was friendly with all the animals, and they counted on him when they were in trouble.

One day, Cody found a magnificent golden eagle named Marahute. Unfortunately, the bird had gotten tangled in a net.

Cody began to cut through the ropes with his pocketknife, and before long, Marahute was free! The eagle gave Cody one of her beautiful golden feathers to show how grateful she was.

While Cody was walking home, the ground suddenly gave way below him. He had fallen into a poacher's trap!

He looked up and saw a tall man peering down at him. It was the greedy Percival McLeach, who captured wild animals and sold them. McLeach was going to let him go, but then he saw the feather. He decided to hold Cody captive until the boy led him to Marahute. The golden eagle was a very rare bird that he could sell for a lot of money.

Luckily, a mouse saw the whole thing and immediately contacted the Rescue Aid Society in New York City. The R.A.S. was an organization of brave mice who helped those in trouble. But there were only two mice courageous enough for this mission: Bernard and Miss Bianca.

Although a blizzard raged in New York, the two mice made their way to the airport. When they arrived, they told their friend Wilbur the albatross that they had to get to Australia—and fast!

At first, Wilbur was reluctant to make the trip. "Have you looked outside?" he asked. "I'm afraid your jolly little holiday will have to wait."

But when Miss Bianca told him about Cody's kidnapping, Wilbur quickly changed his mind. "Nobody takes away a kid's freedom while I'm around!" he declared. The mice got onto Wilbur's back and took off. They had made many daring rescues before, but they had never traveled this far from home.

When they arrived in Australia, Bernard and Miss Bianca surveyed the barren landscape. Which way should they go to find Cody?

Luckily, a rugged kangaroo mouse named Jake showed up. "So, which way are you taking—Suicide Trail through Nightmare Canyon or the shortcut at Satan's Ridge?"

Bernard gulped nervously and looked at his map. *None* of the places Jake had mentioned was on it.

"A map's no good in the outback," said Jake. "What you really need is someone who knows the territory."

Since no one knew the outback better than Jake, he became their guide. He began by rounding up their first ride—a flying squirrel!

Then Jake lassoed a giant python, who carried them on the next leg of their journey. By night, the three mice traveled on the backs of lightning bugs.

Meanwhile, McLeach tried to get Cody to reveal the location of Marahute's nest. He wanted the golden eagle *and* her eggs. When Cody refused, McLeach locked him in a cage. But the boy still wouldn't talk to the poacher.

By the time Miss Bianca, Bernard, and Jake reached McLeach's hideout, the poacher was shoving Cody outside. "Get out of here!" McLeach yelled. "Your bird is dead. Someone shot her."

"Noooo!" cried Cody. He couldn't believe what he was hearing.

"I heard it on the radio this morning," said McLeach. "And she could've been mine if it weren't for you." The poacher's eyes gleamed with evil. "Too bad about those eggs. They'll never survive without their mother."

Cody didn't know that McLeach was lying to get him to go straight to the nest.

Cody ran as fast as his legs would carry him. He had to save Marahute's eggs! The mice watched as McLeach started his big truck, a bushwhacker, and prepared to follow Cody.

Quickly, the mice scooted under the truck. It rumbled along to a high cliff at the edge of a canyon.

McLeach stopped the truck.

The mice looked up and saw Cody climbing to the eagle's nest. They hurried after him as quickly as they could.

"You're in great danger!" Miss Bianca told Cody when she, Bernard, and Jake caught up to him.

But a squawk echoed through the canyon and drowned out her warning.

"Marahute!" cried Cody. He was thrilled and relieved to find that the golden eagle was actually alive.

"Cody, please!" begged Miss Bianca. "You must listen."

"McLeach is on the cliff!" Bernard explained.

Suddenly, Cody understood what the mice had been trying to tell him. McLeach had tricked him, and now Marahute was in danger.

"Marahute, turn back!" cried Cody.

But it was too late. McLeach had attached a net to the bushwhacker's crane and used it to catch the eagle.

Cody was determined to save Marahute, though. He jumped off the cliff and grabbed ahold of the net.

Quickly, Jake lassoed the boy's foot. He and Bianca held on to the rope and were carried along with Cody as the crane moved.

Bernard did not reach the rope in time. "Bianca!" he shouted. He watched as she was lowered into the cage of the bushwhacker along with Cody, Marahute, and Jake.

When McLeach dumped his prisoners into the bushwhacker's cage, he was surprised to see that he had captured more than just the eagle.

"You're in big trouble," Cody warned. "I'll tell the Rangers where you are!"

McLeach, however, had *no* plans to let the boy go.

As soon as Bernard had made sure Marahute's eggs were safe, he began to chase the truck. He saw a wild boar and bravely climbed onto its head. The boar began running through the outback.

At last, Bernard spotted the bushwhacker near Croc Falls. McLeach had tied up Cody and was dangling him over the river from a crane. Hungry crocodiles waited in the water below! *Snap! Snap! Snap!* Their jaws opened and closed as they waited to be fed.

"Now, *this* is my idea of fun," McLeach said, as he got ready to lower Cody into the water.

Suddenly, the bushwhacker's engine went dead. Bernard had stolen the keys! The crane stopped moving, but Cody was still hanging from it.

"Look, it's Bernard!" Miss Bianca cried from inside the cage.

"Way to go, mate!" cheered Jake.

Bernard threw the keys to them. But now poor Bernard had a bigger, slimier problem. . . .

McLeach had brought a lizard with him, and it had spotted Bernard. It began to chase the little mouse around at full speed. But Bernard had an idea. "Oh, my gosh, I hope I know what I'm doing!" he cried. Then he headed straight for McLeach and jumped out of the way at the last second.

Smack! The lizard collided with the poacher, and both of them fell into the river.

Just then, the rope that held Cody snapped. Still tied up, he splashed into the water.

"Bernard!" cried Miss Bianca. "The boy!"

Bernard spotted Cody and leaped into the water, but the current was too strong. It pulled them—and McLeach—toward a waterfall.

McLeach and the lizard went over the edge of the thundering falls. Bernard and Cody were close behind. Soon they were carried over the falls, too!

Then, all of a sudden, they were going up, not down! They found themselves on Marahute's back, along with Miss Bianca and Jake. The eagle had swooped down and saved them! They were safe!

Cody hugged the great eagle, and Miss Bianca hugged Bernard. It had been another great adventure—and another amazing rescue!

DISNEY'S
ROBIN HOOD
The Jailbreak

In Sherwood Forest, there lived two thieves. One was named Robin Hood and the other was called Little John. They were no ordinary outlaws—they stole from the rich to give to the poor.

It all began when the good King Richard left to fight in a war, and his greedy brother, Prince John, took over as ruler. Prince John was only interested in becoming rich, so he ordered the Sheriff of Nottingham to collect as much tax money as he could.

The people of the kingdom became poor and hungry. Robin Hood realized that something had to be done. He knew that King Richard would never have allowed his people to go without food. So he and his friend Little John began to steal.

The prince was determined to capture Robin Hood. But Robin and Little John were very good at tricking Prince John and the Sheriff. No matter how many traps were set, the outlaws always escaped.

Prince John decided the only way to get even with Robin Hood was to collect more money from the poor. "Triple the taxes!" he ordered. "Squeeze every last drop out of those peasants!"

The evil sheriff was only too happy to follow orders. Those who couldn't pay were sent to jail.

Before long, the entire town of Nottingham seemed to be locked in jail: the owls, the mice, the rooster, and all the rabbits. Even Robin's friend Friar Tuck was taken to prison and sentenced to death for treason!

Robin Hood and Little John were shocked when they heard about Friar Tuck's fate. "A jailbreak tonight is the only chance he's got," Robin said.

"A jailbreak?" replied Little John. "There's no way you can get in there."

"We've got to, or Friar Tuck dies at dawn!" Robin told him. He began to plan a daring rescue.

In the middle of the night, Robin Hood and Little John climbed a ladder and surveyed the castle grounds. Five hefty rhinos and some vultures were guarding the jail. Wolf archers patrolled nearby. It was going to be a tough rescue!

Little John snuck up to one of the vultures, captured him, and quietly tied him to a nearby tree. Then Robin Hood put on the guard's outfit so that he could walk around the castle without making anyone suspicious.

"Just you watch this performance," Robin said to Little John.

"Be careful," Little John warned him.

As the lazy sheriff snoozed, Robin carefully stole his keys and gave them to Little John. "You release Friar Tuck and the others," he whispered. "I'll drop in on the royal treasury."

Robin was determined to get back the money that Prince John had taken from the people of the kingdom.

Little John ran up the stairs to the jail cell and began to unlock the prisoners' chains and shackles.

Friar Tuck was so happy he could hardly contain himself. "It can't be!" he exclaimed.

"Shhh! Quiet!" said Little John. "We're busting out of here!"

Meanwhile, Robin Hood went to the tower where the prince was sleeping.

He climbed up a rope and peered through the window. Prince John was asleep inside, a bag of money in each hand. Sir Hiss, a snake who was the prince's adviser, slept at the foot of the bed. Bags and bags of money were piled around the room.

Robin Hood tiptoed into the prince's room. He quietly set up a pulley system that went to the window of the jail below, where Little John and the newly freed prisoners were waiting. Robin attached the moneybags to the ropes, and Little John pulled them toward him. One by one, the bags disappeared from the room.

When Robin was about to leave, he noticed a bag right next to Prince John. He got it, snuck over to the window, and grabbed on to the pulley rope.

Sir Hiss woke up just as Robin was leaving. The snake grabbed one of the moneybags on the rope. Then he wrapped his tail around Prince John's foot. When the bag moved along the pulley, it pulled Sir Hiss and the prince—and his bed—with it! Hiss and Prince John went sliding across the room. *Blam!*—the bed slammed into the balcony.

The prince clung to the balcony railing for dear life. *"Ahhh!"* he screamed.

Robin was still on the pulley.

"*Guards!*" yelled the prince. "My gold!"

The guards unleashed a flurry of arrows. Robin moved along the rope, dodging the arrows. When the outlaw reached the jail, the prince fell to the ground with a *splat*. Still, he ordered the guards to go after Robin.

Little John and the
prisoners ran toward the
drawbridge, clutching the
prince's gold, with Robin
Hood close behind. When
the guards' arrows flew
toward them, Robin shot

back a few arrows of his own. Then some of the rhinos charged.
Luckily, Little John spotted a cart filled with barrels. He emptied it,
and the barrels slammed into the guards, knocking them over.

The prisoners loaded the gold onto the cart and jumped in.
Robin Hood lowered the drawbridge. Little John and Friar Tuck
moved the cart across—they were almost out of the castle!

But before Robin could catch up with them, a guard cut a rope,
and a giant metal gate crashed down in front of him.

Robin Hood was trapped!

Robin told his friends to go ahead—he'd catch up with them later.

The Sheriff ran toward the gate. "We've got him now," he boasted to his rhino guards.

They charged, but Robin was quick on his feet. He swiftly climbed the gate, grabbed a rope, and swung right into the Sheriff, knocking him into a second line of guards. Robin then swung to the top of the castle wall and ran along it.

The angry sheriff chased him up to the castle tower. He tried to strike Robin with a flaming torch but set fire to the curtains and rug instead!

Robin tried to defend himself, but as the fire filled the room, he was forced to flee up the stairs to the top of the tower. Before long, the fire snaked up the stairs, and soon the flames were biting at his feet. There was only one way out—he'd have to jump.

With no other choice, Robin Hood bravely climbed out the window and scurried up the spire atop the tower.

His friends watched nervously from the shore, hoping that Robin was all right.

Prince John ordered his guards to shoot at the trapped outlaw.

Robin took a heroic leap and jumped into the moat far below. Guards fired arrows into the water, hoping to hit him.

But no one could catch the clever Robin Hood. Avoiding the arrows, he swam to safety and rejoined his friends.

The jailbreak had been a success! The people of the kingdom were free, and they had gotten their hard-earned money back.

Soon King Richard returned and fixed everything. The king even declared that Robin Hood was no longer an outlaw.

Now Robin was free for another adventure . . . to marry his sweetheart, Maid Marian!

As for Prince John . . . he and his partners in crime were sentenced to hard labor. Now, instead of sorting through piles of money, they sorted through piles of rocks. Robin Hood and the people of the kingdom couldn't imagine anything more fitting.

DISNEY'S
Lilo & Stitch
Tons of Trouble

In a faraway galaxy, an alien scientist named Jumba Jukiba made a one-of-a-kind creature called Experiment 626. The creature's dangerous, destructive ways quickly landed him—and Jumba—in prison.

Soon 626 escaped and headed to planet Earth!

The Grand Councilwoman ordered Jumba and his new partner, Pleakley, to capture 626 and bring him back. In exchange, Jumba would no longer be imprisoned.

But 626 had a plan of his own . . . and it did *not* involve being captured. He ended up in an animal-rescue center on the Hawaiian island of Kauai. He hid his spikes, antennae, and extra legs and pretended to be a dog.

A while later, a little girl named Lilo and her older sister, Nani, went to the animal-rescue center to find a pet.

"Go pick someone out," Nani said to her sister.

Lilo walked past the counter toward the kennel. When she saw 626, she knew she had to have him.

"What is that thing?" Nani cried when her sister and 626 appeared in the waiting area.

"A dog, I think," the rescue lady answered nervously.

"His name is . . . Stitch," Lilo announced.

Outside the rescue center, Jumba and Pleakley watched closely. They knew they had to capture Stitch at just the right moment—without harming any humans.

After Lilo spent the day trying to train Stitch, the two went to the restaurant where Nani worked.

Lilo tried to tell Stitch how bad he'd been. But he was more interested in eating cake. Then he smelled something. He followed the scent to a table of tourists.

"Aha!" one of the tourists cried, grabbing hold of Stitch. It was Jumba in disguise!

Stitch tried to free himself, but it was no use. Finally, Stitch unhinged his jaw and pretended to eat Pleakley's head! When Nani finally pulled Stitch off of Pleakley, he wrangled free and ran back to Lilo.

Nani lost her job because of Stitch's stunt, but that was just the beginning.

When they got home, Lilo told Stitch, "This is a great home. You'll like it a lot!" She gave him a pillow so he could feel how soft it was, but he just shredded it.

In the kitchen, Stitch pulled the blender off the counter and examined it curiously. The glass jar was filled with a pink liquid. He turned the blender on.

"Hey, what are you doing?" Lilo asked.

Stitch removed the lid to look inside the jar. *Splash!* The liquid mixture went all over Stitch, who thought the blender was attacking him. He wrestled with it and got the pink liquid all over the kitchen.

Later that night, Lilo took Stitch up to her room. She pointed to a cardboard box with a pillow and blanket tucked inside it. "This is your bed," she told him.

Stitch wasn't interested in sleeping in a box, so he climbed into Lilo's bed. Next, he grabbed a precious picture of her parents, took her favorite doll, and ruined one of her drawings.

Finally, Lilo said, "You wreck everything you touch. Why not try and *make* something for a change?"

Within minutes, Stitch created a little city from objects in Lilo's room. But once he was done, he knocked it over.

"No more caffeine for you!" Lilo decided.

The next day, Nani went to look for a new job. A social worker named Cobra Bubbles had been watching Nani and Lilo. He told Nani that if she couldn't take care of Lilo, he would have to take her sister away.

While Nani applied for a job at the local grocery store, Lilo decided to teach Stitch how to behave. First, she showed him how to dance.

Unfortunately, their dance routine knocked the grocery store owner into a fruits and vegetables display . . . so Nani didn't get that job.

Next, Nani applied for a job at a coffee shop. Lilo continued with Stitch's lessons. She handed Stitch a ukulele. But when he played it, the high notes shattered the windows of the coffee shop. Thanks to Stitch, Nani didn't get that job, either. Things didn't look good.

Stitch realized that he was making life worse for Lilo and Nani, so he decided to leave. He spent the night outside. By morning, he realized how important Lilo was to him.

He started to go back, but just then, Jumba cornered him, "Don't run!" ordered Jumba. "Come quietly."

That wasn't Stitch's style, though. He ran toward the house.

"Come back here!" Jumba yelled as he tore through the trees with his plasma blaster.

Stitch entered through the dog door and led Lilo out of the line of fire.

Jumba burst in and began a furious battle with Stitch. Furniture was destroyed left and right.

Frightened, Lilo ran to the phone and called Cobra Bubbles. "Aliens are attacking my house!" she cried. "They want my dog!" Lilo didn't know what to do.

Suddenly, the house began to shake. *Bam!* Stitch smashed through the wall, carrying a car. He walloped Jumba with it, but the alien just shook it off.

Before long, the entire house was destroyed. Soon Cobra Bubbles and Nani arrived. While Cobra and Nani argued about what would happen to Lilo, the little girl ran into the forest. Stitch followed her.

Wanting to apologize, Stitch handed Lilo a photo of her family, which he had managed to find amid the remains of the house.

"You ruined everything!" she cried, taking the photo.

Then Stitch transformed back into his original alien shape.

Lilo began to understand that he had never been a dog, that he was really an alien. "You're one of them?" she asked, not quite believing it.

At that moment, an alien named Captain Gantu appeared. He had been sent by the Grand Councilwoman to finish the job Jumba and Pleakley had started: catching Stitch.

Being twenty feet tall, Captain Gantu easily captured Stitch with a net. But he also trapped Lilo!

Gantu was very proud of his triumph. "And here I thought you'd be difficult to catch," he told Stitch with a smirk. "Silly me."

Gantu put Lilo and Stitch into a containment pod on the back of his ship. As the captain went into the cockpit to power up the ship, Stitch began his escape. He popped out of the pod and climbed on top of it to try and free Lilo. Before Stitch could get a grip, though, the ship's main engines fired and sent him crashing to the ground.

The spaceship took off—with Lilo aboard!

Nani arrived just as the spaceship flew into the sky. "Lilo!" she cried.

Wham! Something hard made contact with Stitch's head. He looked up to see Nani holding a thick branch.

"Okay, talk! I know you had something to do with this!" she said to Stitch. "Now, where's Lilo? *Talk!* I know you can!"

Before he could respond, Stitch was slammed by a plasma blast and handcuffed by Jumba. But that didn't stop Nani. She pleaded with the aliens for their help. In the end, it was actually Stitch who persuaded Jumba and Pleakley to help rescue the little girl.

Nani and the three aliens took off in Jumba's huge red spaceship. Before long, they caught up to Gantu's ship, and a great battle began. Gantu was shocked that Stitch had freed himself. He fired on Jumba's spaceship, forcing Jumba to turn sideways and use the lush, green mountains for cover.

"Hold on!" yelled Jumba as he made another quick turn. He swung the ship back around and hit Gantu's spacecraft.

Stitch then jumped onto Gantu's ship to rescue Lilo. Soon Captain Gantu was defeated and Lilo was freed.

Once everyone was safely back on the ground, it was decided that Stitch could stay on Earth and that Lilo could stay with Nani. Everyone could see that Stitch had finally learned what family was all about . . . and how to stay out of trouble.

Alien Invasion

Chicken Little was tired of everyone laughing at him. It all started when something fell from the sky and hit him on the head. "The sky is falling!" he'd yelled. His warning caused a panic in Oakey Oaks, the town that he lived in. When he told everyone what happened, no one believed him—not even his dad, Buck. They all thought an acorn had fallen from an oak tree and hit him. Since then, he had been known as "that crazy little chicken."

Life was just getting back to normal when part of the sky fell again—right into Chicken Little's bedroom. He thought it looked like some sort of panel. *"Nooo!"* he cried. This couldn't be happening again!

"What's wrong?" asked his dad, bursting into the room.

"Nothing," replied Chicken Little. "I, uh . . . fell out of bed!" He quickly hid the panel. If anyone found out he thought the sky had fallen again, life would be awful.

As soon as his father left, Chicken Little called his friends Abby, Runt, and Fish and begged them to come over.

"I'm sure there's a simple explanation," Abby said when she saw the panel. "It could be a piece of a weather balloon, or maybe it's part of some experimental communications satellite."

"I don't care what it is," Chicken Little announced. "Are you gonna help me get rid of it or not?"

While the others tried to figure out a plan, Fish climbed on top of the panel. To everyone's surprise, it floated off the floor and zoomed out the window!

"Come on!" cried Chicken Little. He and his pals raced outside and chased after Fish.

The panel came to a stop over the baseball stadium. Suddenly, a bright light filled the sky, and a spaceship appeared! Chicken Little and Runt ran for shelter in the dugout—but Abby was too scared to move.

"C'mon, let's get out of here!" Chicken Little yelled. He grabbed Abby's arm and pulled her to safety just as the spaceship landed.

While the friends watched, two spidery-looking aliens dropped out of the hatch and scuttled off.

"Poor Fish!" Runt cried. "He's gone!"

"Not yet," said Abby. She pointed to the top of the ship. There was Fish, waving happily.

Chicken Little, Abby, and Runt climbed aboard the spaceship to rescue Fish. Inside, it was dark and creepy. Eerie lights zapped on and off, and tentacles hung down from the ceiling.

The only friendly sight was a cute, fuzzy orange creature floating in a beam of light. Chicken Little stopped and winked at it, and the alien winked back. Then it hopped down and quietly followed Chicken Little.

"Where are you, Fish?" Runt whispered frantically. All the spooky sights and sounds were making him very nervous.

Suddenly, Fish jumped out from behind a screen. He was just fine.

"All right, let's get out of here," Abby ordered. But now Runt was missing!

Fish pointed to a room down the hall. Runt was staring up at the ceiling with a terrified look on his face. A giant picture of the entire solar system was on the wall. Several planets were crossed out, but Earth was circled and arrows were pointed at it. It looked like the aliens were going to destroy the planet!

"We're running back to your house, and you're going to tell your dad," Abby said.

Chicken Little agreed. Meanwhile, the aliens had returned to the ship and discovered that the

fuzzy orange creature was missing. The aliens saw Chicken Little and his pals and assumed they'd taken it!

Chicken Little, Abby, Runt, and Fish left the ship and ran into the forest. The aliens were right behind them and catching up fast! The friends accidentally tumbled down a hill into a cornfield. They crouched down among the stalks as the aliens shined flashlights over the field.

Bzzz! Bzzz! Bzzz! Spinning blades came out of the aliens' arms, and they began to chop down row upon row of corn, still trying to find Chicken Little and his friends. The aliens were right next to them! If they wanted to live, the friends had to leave the cornfield— and fast!

"Hurry!" urged Chicken Little. As the four zigzagged through the field, trying to make their escape, Abby realized there was no time to waste.

"We've got to ring the school bell to warn everyone!" she cried.

Chicken Little and the others dashed out of the field. They knew they didn't have much time before the aliens caught up with them. But when they reached the school, the doors were locked!

Thinking quickly, Chicken Little used a fizzy bottle of soda to rocket himself to the bell tower. Then he grabbed the rope and pulled the bell with all his might. *Ding-dong! Ding-dong!*

The aliens fled back to their ship just as the alarmed townspeople gathered at the school. Everyone thought Chicken Little had imagined the whole thing—just like he had imagined that the sky was falling.

"Dad," pleaded Chicken Little, "I'm not making this up. You gotta believe me this time!"

"No, son, I don't," Buck answered.

Later, as Chicken Little sat in his yard, the little orange alien that had been following him showed up. Luckily, Fish came by, too. He could understand the creature's language. It turned out the alien's name was Kirby, and he had been left behind by the spaceship.

"Don't cry," said Chicken Little reassuringly. "We'll do whatever it takes to get you back home."

Just then, the sky began to rumble and crack into pieces. Rubble poured down like hail. Buck and the rest of the town ran outside to see what was the matter. They couldn't believe what they saw: a fleet of spaceships hovered over the town hall. Oakey Oaks was being invaded by aliens!

Instantly, the town erupted in panic. Screams filled the air as the people of Oakey Oaks fled anywhere they could.

"It's just a rescue mission," Chicken Little explained to his father. He told Buck about Kirby and asked his dad to help him reunite the little alien with his parents.

Buck finally realized that Chicken Little had been telling the truth all along. "Just tell me what you need me to do," he said.

By now, things in Oakey Oaks had gotten even worse. Aliens were dropping out of their ships and vaporizing everything in their paths! Even so, Buck listened to his son's plan.

"All we have to do is duck and weave through traffic," Chicken Little said, "and make our way through the town square while avoiding death rays from those alien robots. Then we get to the town hall, climb up to the highest point on the roof, and give the kid back to its parents."

Buck agreed—he trusted his son.

Buck, Kirby, and Chicken Little drove through town quickly, moving right and left to dodge the aliens' vaporizing rays. When they finally reached the town hall, one of the angry creatures blocked their path.

"Okay, son," said Buck. "Now what?"

Just then, Runt zipped by in a fire truck and pulled them aboard. He raced to the town hall and Buck, Chicken Little, and Kirby went up to the building's domed rooftop.

"Here's your kid!" shouted Chicken Little, holding Kirby up to the spaceship.

A beam of light shot down from the ship and instantly transported Buck, Kirby, and Chicken Little inside. A huge image of an angry, three-eyed alien confronted them. "Why did you take our child?" it boomed.

Buck tried to explain that it had all been a harmless misunderstanding, but the big red alien was not convinced.

"You have violated intergalactic law 90210, a charge punishable by immediate particle disintegration," the voice said.

Luckily, Kirby explained that Buck was telling the truth. Just then, two scary, spidery-looking aliens appeared. Their armor opened up to reveal two small, furry aliens who looked just like Kirby. They were his parents, Melvin and Tina. Melvin had used a special screen and microphone to make himself seem big and scary.

He explained how the aliens came to Earth every year to gather acorns— and that Oakey Oaks had the best ones in the universe.

Then the aliens unvaporized what they had destroyed, and everything was back to normal. As they started to leave—*clunk!*—a blue panel fell off their ship.

"Every time we come here this thing falls off," complained Tina. "Someday, it's gonna hit somebody on the head."

"Nonsense!" replied Melvin. "The chances of that happening are a million to one!"

Chicken Little knew just how wrong Melvin was. He and his dad looked at each other as the alien family's spaceship took off. Maybe life would finally get back to normal.

Goofy Blasts Off

It was a beautiful, clear night. Goofy had just gotten a new telescope and was eager to show it to Mickey Mouse. "Gawrsh," he said to himself as he walked toward his friend's house, "it's a perfect night for looking at stars and planets!"

"You're just in time," Mickey said when Goofy arrived.

"I am?" Goofy asked.

"I'm on my way to see Pluto," Mickey explained.

"You are?" Goofy asked. He couldn't believe it—Mickey wanted to look at the planets, too!

"Sure," said Mickey. "You can come along. Why don't you wait on the porch while I get the car?"

Goofy sat down on the porch swing and gazed at the sky. "I wonder which one of those cute little twinkly lights is Pluto." Suddenly, he felt very sleepy. "Boy, I sure hope we don't have to drive too far to set up the telescope," he said, yawning.

Beep! Beep!

Goofy rubbed his eyes. Then he shook his head and jumped to his feet. Mickey was in his car. But it didn't really look like a car.

Goofy ran down the steps and hopped into the car. There were monitors and buttons everywhere.

305

"Gawrsh, Mickey," Goofy said, "your car looks just like a spaceship!"

"That's because it *is* a spaceship," said Mickey.

Oh, we really *are* going to visit Pluto, Goofy said to himself.

"Welcome aboard!" crackled a voice in the control panel.

"Thanks!" Goofy replied. "Hey, who said that?"

"That's PAL," said Mickey, "our computer pilot." Then he started the countdown. "Ten . . . nine . . . eight . . . seven . . . six . . . five . . . four . . ." The rockets roared to life. ". . . three . . . two . . . one . . . *blastoff!*" The spaceship shot upward. Before long, they were in space.

"How far away is Pluto, anyway?" Goofy asked.

"Let's ask PAL!" Mickey suggested.

"Pluto is a dwarf planet that's nearly four billion miles away," the computer said.

"We better step on it, then," said Goofy. "Mickey, can't you make this buggy go any faster?"

"Sure thing, Goofy!" Mickey replied. He pressed a button on the control panel. "Hold on!"

"*Whoaaaaaaaaa!*" cried Mickey and Goofy as the spaceship zoomed forward.

"L-l-look!" said Goofy. He pointed at a bright light up ahead. "Somebody left a l-l-light on."

"Alert," PAL announced. "We are now approaching the sun. Its surface temperature is 10,000 degrees. Activate brakes immediately!"

Screeech! The spaceship slid to a stop as Mickey slammed on the brakes.

"Now what?" Goofy asked.

"I think we better turn this ship around," Mickey replied.

Soon the ship was speeding in the other direction. Before long, it passed Mercury and Venus. In the distance, Goofy and Mickey saw a blue planet with brown patches and white swirls.

"I'd know that planet anywhere!" Mickey cried. "It's Earth!"

"Do you think we can see our houses from up here?" Goofy asked.

Mickey laughed. "I think we're a little too far away."

Back on course again, Goofy and Mickey passed by a dry, red planet that was covered with craters, mountains, and valleys. It was Mars. Mickey and Goofy were staring at it when, suddenly, there was a big *klunk!* The spaceship shook and rattled.

"PAL!" cried Mickey. "What's happening?"

"We are now passing through an asteroid belt," PAL replied.

"An asteroid belt?" asked Goofy. "Gawrsh, I didn't even know that asteroids wore pants."

"They don't," PAL explained. "Asteroids are chunks of rock and metal that orbit the sun between Mars and Jupiter. A belt is just an area with lots of asteroids."

Bonk! Bam! More asteroids slammed into the ship and flipped it upside down.

Klunk! Another asteroid hit them and turned the ship right side up. Luckily, Mickey was able to guide the ship through the asteroid belt.

"Golly!" Mickey said when he saw the next planet. "It's huge! Is that Pluto?"

"That is Jupiter—the largest planet in the solar system," PAL replied.

As Mickey steered the spaceship past Jupiter, Saturn came into view. It was encircled by seven brightly colored rings.

"The rings are made of millions of pieces of ice, rock, and dust," PAL announced.

"Look at the ice on the spaceship!" Goofy cried.

"It's cold here, all right," Mickey answered. Then he checked the speedometer on the control panel.

312

"Gee, Goofy, we're already more than one and a half billion miles from home."

"Gawrsh," Goofy said, "that's really far!"

Before long, the friends zipped past two more planets, Uranus and Neptune.

"The spaceship is now approaching Pluto," PAL announced.

"You mean we're finally here?" Goofy asked.

"Affirmative," PAL responded.

Goofy decided to take a space walk.

"Don't forget your mittens and scarf," Mickey told him. "It's cold out there."

"That is correct," said PAL. "The temperature on the surface of Pluto is 360 degrees below zero."

313

"Hey, Mickey!" called Goofy as he floated through space. "This is more like a space *swim* than a space walk!"

Goofy decided to take a closer look at Pluto. He jabbed at a button on his space suit. "I bet this will get me closer."

"Warning!" PAL cautioned. "The jet pack has been activated."

Flames roared out of Goofy's jet pack.

He went spinning and tumbling through space. Goofy was headed straight for the surface of Pluto!

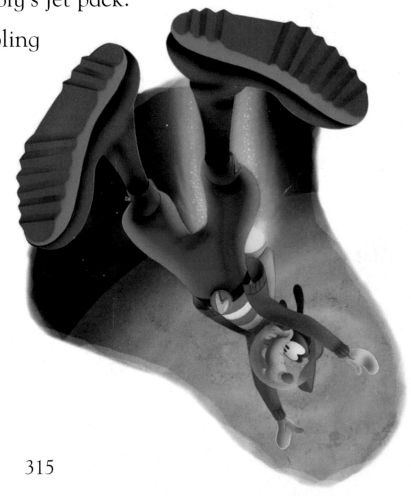

"Mickey!" he yelled as he zoomed away from his friend. *"Helllllp!"* But Mickey was too far away.

How would Goofy ever get back to the spaceship?

315

"Gooooofy!" a voice called. It was Mickey, but it sounded like he was very far away. *Beep! Beep!* It was the spaceship horn!

Goofy's eyes blinked open. Mickey was sitting in his car, not in the spaceship.

"Gawrsh," Goofy said, looking around. He was on the porch swing, not in space. "What's going on? I thought we were visiting Pluto."

"We *are* visiting Pluto," said Mickey. "He's at the animal hospital with a sore paw. Come on, let's go."

"Ohhh, your dog Pluto, not the Pluto in space," Goofy said.

At the hospital, Pluto jumped up and barked happily when he saw them. He was feeling much better and was ready to go home.

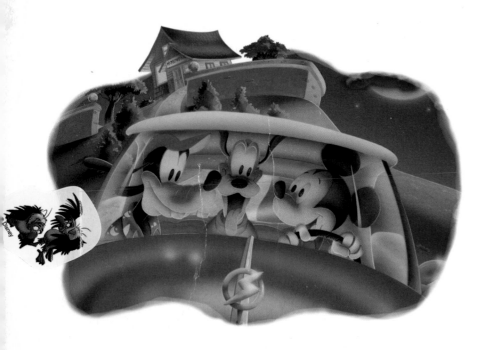

On the drive home, Goofy began to talk about their trip to space.

"You must have been dreaming," said Mickey. "But we can use my car to go see outer space. I'll show you."

Mickey drove all the way to the top of Lookout Hill. Then he helped Goofy set up his new telescope.

"Gawrsh!" Goofy cried when he looked into the telescope. "You're right, Mickey! I can see the planets and stars really well."

"You got to see two Plutos in one day," Mickey remarked.

Goofy grinned. What a great adventure he'd had—even if most of it had been in his sleep!